Puffin Books
Editor: Kaye Webb

THE FUNNY GUY

'I'm not funny and I'm not a guy,' said Helen out loud to her reflection in the mirror, but she shouldn't have done it. Before she could move away or even turn round, Susan Johnson's pretty face peered over her shoulder. 'Oh yes, you are,' she said. 'You're the Funny Guy – the Funny Guy,' and she pulled a horrible face.

Two years ago, before her mother had her accident and went to hospital, there had been nothing funny about Helen. She'd been just an ordinary girl, quite happy at school and at home. It was afterwards, with Father so worried and often away visiting Mother, that Helen got lonely and started doing funny absent-minded things at school, things that made her look silly in front of the others.

How Helen longed to be an ordinary girl with an ordinary mother waiting for her at home. And how she longed, when her twelfth birthday came, to have a bicycle for her present. But it didn't happen. Poor Mother was worse than ever. 'I know you will help me by being brave and patient,' wrote her father from the city, and Helen *did* try hard – until she cooked up the fatal scheme that landed her in disgrace for the rest of the summer . . .

Everyone who has ever suffered the miseries of being the odd one out will sympathize with Helen, and feel almost as delighted as she does when at last her luck begins to change for the better.

For readers of ten and ov

Grace Allen Hogarth

The Funny Guy

Illustrated by Fritz Wegner

Puffin Books

Puffin Books, Penguin Books Ltd, Harmondsworth, Middlesex, England
Penguin Books Australia Ltd, Ringwood, Victoria, Australia
Penguin Books (N.Z.) Ltd, 182–190 Wairau Road, Auckland 10, New Zealand

First published by Hamish Hamilton 1955
Published in Puffin Books 1975
Copyright © Grace Allen Hogarth, 1955

—

Made and printed in Great Britain by
Cox & Wyman Ltd, London, Reading and Fakenham
Set in Intertype Baskerville

Contents

CHAPTER ONE

The Funny Guy

THE front door slammed behind Helen Hamilton. 'It would,' she said to herself, and then again, 'It just would.' She stood still for a moment to see how serious the noise had been and what effects it would have. In the large maple tree that hung over the porch, birds were having their cheerful early morning conversations; but the house was silent. It was all right then. Auntie Cris must be in the kitchen and her father wouldn't bother to put down his paper and come out just to scold her. He wasn't like that at all. Whenever she forgot and thundered down the stairs, he would say, 'Quietly, Nelly, quietly – ' and smile at her in a tired way so that she would try hard to remember the next time. No, it was only Auntie Cris who would scold and, thank goodness, this time, Auntie Cris hadn't heard.

If only the front door wasn't so heavy and the wind that seemed to push from behind so strong, she would have time to remember. But there were always so many other things to think about, and on this bright April morning there were even more things than usual.

There was, first of all, the bicycle. There were only eight more days to wait. Today was April the second, and on April the tenth she would be twelve years old.

'Twelve years old – twelve years old,' she chanted to herself as she skipped along the sidewalk under the budding trees. And then, 'A bicycle – a bicycle – all for my very own – '

She looked up at the bits of blue sky through the

branches overhead and thought of what her father had said at breakfast. He had been smiling as he stirred his coffee.

'On a lovely April morning like this, Helen, I can't help thinking of your birthday – the very day, I mean – And at the hospital in Newton, Massachusetts, U.S.A.'

'Just at the turn of the century,' Helen put in quickly.

Her father laughed and put down his spoon as Auntie Cris bustled in and put his boiled egg in front of him with a small clattering noise.

'Don't interrupt, Helen,' she said crisply.

Helen thought that Auntie Cris was interrupting herself, but she managed not to say so. It was hard to be looked after by an aunt instead of a mother. And it was even harder when it wasn't a real aunt but just Auntie Cris. Helen watched her father's slow, sure hands as he broke his egg into the cup, and went on quietly, 'Yes, it's easy to remember how old you are; one year old in nineteen hundred and one – two in nineteen hundred and two – '

'Three in nineteen hundred and three,' Helen couldn't help saying.

'Yes – all the way to TWELVE – a very great age – in nineteen hundred and twelve. April the tenth. That is, let me see – '

'A week from tomorrow, Daddy. And you promised that you would be home for supper – and that I could have Barbara Buckingham, too – '

'That's the order of the day, is it? And your mother is so much better, Helen – so very much better – that perhaps we can have a real celebration this year – '

It was then that Auntie Cris made the rumbling noise in her throat that usually came before she said something fierce or cross. But this time she didn't say anything because Mr Hamilton leaned across the table and very neatly dropped his eggshell into her coffee cup, where it bobbed up and down on its little brown lake.

Helen shrieked with joy. How did he dare? How did he ever dare? But he did, of course, he dared to do anything. All the same, he hadn't played that game with Auntie Cris for years and years – not since Helen had been a little girl – not for two years anyway – not since her mother's accident. She held her breath to see if he had forgotten what came next. But he hadn't. He said slowly, 'Why, Mrs McCrillis, whatever has happened to your coffee?' He looked up to the ceiling.

'Oh, Daddy, the sky is falling – the sky is falling,' Helen cried.

And then Auntie Cris smiled one of her rare good smiles. 'Small boys must play their disgusting tricks,' she said, with just the right sound of school-teacher fierceness. 'And some small boys never do grow up, Mr Hamilton.'

She removed the eggshell as if it were alive and horrid to hold like the old toad in the garden. Then she looked over her half-spectacles at Helen. 'Eat up your breakfast, dear, or you'll be late for school – '

That was the end of the game but Auntie Cris had called her 'dear'. Oh, yes, it had been a very good breakfast, just like all the breakfasts before her mother had been taken away to hospital. Auntie Cris hadn't lived with them then, of course, but she used to come sometimes to stay for a week or two and do all the mending and help with the housework. She'd been really cross the first time Helen's father had put his eggshell in her coffee cup, and Helen's mother had looked a little worried. But no one could be cross with Mr Hamilton for long – not even Auntie Cris who could be cross with everyone else for a whole day, especially when the wind was in the east and her rheumatism troubled her.

As Helen turned the corner by the station, she heard the eight-twenty-five train come puffing under the bridge. That meant that she had five minutes to get through the main street where the shops were, past the Congregational Church where she went every Sunday, to the red brick schoolhouse where she was going now.

There would be just time to stop and buy some sweets at Belcher's Store if only she had some pennies. Perhaps, this morning, she could have asked her father for some. He'd been so cheerful that he might just have reached into his pocket without remembering that she'd already had two weeks' pocket money ahead and the fifty cent piece that her mother had given her the last time she had been to the hospital. But if he had remembered and said, 'What's become of all your pocket money and that fifty cents your mother gave you?' then she would have had to tell him how she had spent her own money on sweets and had lost the fifty cent piece out of her apron pocket when she went to show it to Barbara Buckingham. Perhaps he would have frowned and picked up his paper and Auntie Cris would have said, 'Tsch, tsch,' with her teeth clacking or, 'I wonder you trust a child of her age with money at all' – and that would have spoiled breakfast – No, it was much better to do without sweets even if Susan Johnson did have a whole striped bag full of them.

At the thought of Susan Johnson, Helen frowned and tossed back one of her straight black pigtails that had come forward on to her shoulder. Susan Johnson was beautiful. She had long golden curls like Mary Pickford in the movies. She was also rich and wore wonderful clothes, even to school. And it was Susan who had first called Helen the hateful name –

Between the white wooden walls of the Congregational Church and the red brick walls of the school building there was a gap of about fifty yards that was filled in by a high board fence. This separated the road from the play-ground – a wide field that lay like a flat brown and green handkerchief behind the church and the school. It was scuffed brown where the children played games, but under the elm trees, where they sat down to rest and talk and eat apples or sweets, the long grass was green.

As Helen looked at the fence from the road she could see the tall plain boards and the wooden beams running crossways that were fine for climbing. It was easy to stand on the bottom beam and peer over the top or even to climb to the upper one and sit with one's legs hanging over the edge. Helen, herself, had often climbed up during break to watch both sides, like a queen from her castle. You could see the other children playing games and the people passing by in the road. Now, as she passed the church and looked up at the clock in the tower, she saw that it was twenty-six minutes past eight. Four whole minutes before Helen and the other children had to be inside. And, at that very moment, the school bell began to ring. 'Clang – clang – hurry up,' it said, but no one ever paid any attention until the last possible minute. Perhaps Miss Perkins would come out and call them all in. If only she would.

There they were, as Helen had known they would be – a row of faces peering over the top of the fence. She looked sideways at them quickly and saw Robert Busby's carrot-red hair before she looked away again. She mustn't let them think she even noticed. She must hold her head up like a soldier, stare straight ahead, and walk on. She mustn't hurry. She mustn't pay any attention. It was a long way but she must be BRAVE, like William Tell, or Pocahontas.

Ping. Helen felt a sharp pain as the hard little bean from Robert's shooter hit her bare wrist and bounced off. She wanted to rub the hurt place and she wanted to run.

But she didn't. The door of the school looked miles away but she didn't make a dash for it and she didn't once look in the direction of the fence.

Someone shouted, 'The Funny Guy, The Funny Guy – There goes The Funny Guy.'

Ping. Another bean whisked by her ear.

'The Funny Guy. The Funny Guy. There goes The Funny Guy.'

The door of the school stood open and welcoming. Helen fixed her eye on it and walked, slowly, slowly towards it. Another bean hit her shoulder.

This was too much. Helen turned in sudden fury and shook her fist at the faces peering over the fence. 'Cowardy custards. Cowardy custards,' she screamed, 'hiding behind the fence.'

This was what her enemies had been waiting for. The heads ducked down out of sight and loud laughter now came from the direction of the playground.

Anyway they weren't watching now. But Helen didn't care if they were. She made a sudden wild dash for the open, waiting door. Safe inside, she stood for a moment until her legs stopped trembling and then went on into the dressing-room to hang up her coat. She was sure that she had seen Susan's yellow head over the fence and she must, at all costs, get to her desk before Susan came in. Helen took a quick look in the small mirror that hung beside the door. 'I'm not funny and I'm not a guy,' she said out loud to the small snub nose and bright dark eyes that stared back at her, and then before she could move away or even turn around, the pretty face of Susan Johnson peered over her shoulder. 'Oh, yes, you are,' the rose-bud mouth said. 'You're The Funny Guy – The Funny Guy.' A small red tongue shot out, the blue eyes squinted darkly and the golden curls tossed.

'I hate you. I hate you. I hate you,' Helen said wildly as

she swung around and tried to escape. For a moment Susan managed to block Helen's way. Then she pushed past and on through the swing door into the school-room.

'Hurry, girls,' Miss Perkins said quietly, but she did not look up from the pile of papers on her desk.

Helen was just sliding into her seat when Susan walked slowly down the aisle between the desks. She was wearing a new dress, pink, with embroidery around the neck and sleeves. She smoothed it out carefully under her as she sat down.

A moment later, Robert Busby, Clarence Strong, and Arthur Evans came in from the boys' door and scuffed to their places.

Miss Perkins looked up. 'You're very nearly late. Have you been hanging about outside?'

'No, Miss Perkins,' Robert answered. He was always the spokesman – the acknowledged leader of the boys, as Susan was of the girls. 'I had to do an errand for my father on the way to school and Clarence and Arthur waited for me.'

'And what was the errand?' Miss Perkins asked. Helen began to feel better. She turned around to stare at Robert who sat in the corner seat at the back of the room.

'Beans,' Robert answered quickly.

Someone giggled and Miss Perkins frowned. 'Very well, I'll keep them safe for you until the end of school. You can bring them to me' – and then, as Robert made no move to get up, she added – 'at once.'

Robert got slowly to his feet and felt in all his pockets, one after the other. At last he produced a battered paper bag, but it was not until the teacher said, 'All right. Quickly please,' that he walked up the aisle and put it on the desk in front of her.

'Thank you,' Miss Perkins said. She picked up the limp

bag and looked at it for a moment. Then she went on, 'An odd errand for your father, wasn't it? Perhaps I'd better have the shooter as well, just to be on the safe side.'

Robert, who was standing by her desk, again searched his pockets, brought out his bright tin toy and placed it beside the paper bag. He now looked a dull poppy red under his freckles. The class stared, fascinated, as the teacher put Robert's treasures into her drawer and sent him back to his seat. Then the excitement was forgotten as

the bell rang and they shuffled to their feet to salute the American flag that hung over Miss Perkins's desk, as they always did every morning.

Helen stood up with the others and raised her hand to her forehead. But she was thinking: I pledge allegiance to my teacher. She *knows*. I'm sure of it. Tomorrow morning she'll come outside to look. And in eight days I'll have my bicycle. I can keep it in the shed by the kindergarten. Oh, yes. I'll ride it to school and I'll go racing past the old fence – I'll ride and I'll ride and I'll whirl along with the wind whistling by me. I'll show them then. I'll show them I'm not a funny guy.

'Helen,' Miss Perkins said. 'Where are you?'

Helen started. The salute to the flag was finished and the others had sat down while Helen still stood with her arm outstretched and her eyes staring blankly at the stars and stripes over the blackboard.

She sat down quickly and a hot blush made her feel red all over. A desk lid went up behind her and a muffled voice said distinctly, 'The Funny Guy. The Funny Guy. The Funny Guy *again*.'

Helen lifted her desk cover and turned around to stick out her tongue at Clarence. This gave her a moment's satisfaction. Then she felt for the familiar shape of her arithmetic book and the day's work began.

CHAPTER TWO

A Disappointment

WHEN Helen came down the steps from the school on the day before her birthday, she was a little anxious about passing the fence. She usually stayed on after the others had gone, so that she could walk along the main street as far as the station with Miss Perkins who always took the train to go home. It was just too bad that today there had to be a Teachers' Meeting since Helen didn't dare to wait a whole hour after school for fear Auntie Cris would get worried and then be cross and spoil everything. But this afternoon Helen was in luck. As she passed the fence no heads showed over the top and there was no sound of shouting or laughter from the direction of the playground. Perhaps the gang had given her up now that she stayed so often to wipe off the blackboards and help Miss Perkins. If only she could be sure of it, that would be one good thing; and the mornings were better now, too, because if Helen got to the church at twenty-seven minutes past eight, Miss Perkins came out on the door step and called the others in, just in time.

Helen skipped a little, practising with both feet, but the left one still wasn't as good a skipper as the right. Then she thought about how much she loved Miss Perkins and she began to hum the tune that Mr Walton had been teaching them that morning, 'Oh beautiful for spacious skies – '. She looked up at the small clouds chasing each other about like woolly lambs. She was sure Miss Perkins knew about Helen's trouble with Robert and Susan and the others; but in all their time after school and in their walks to the station, they talked about other things.

As she went on thinking about Miss Perkins, Helen stopped humming and began to wish that she didn't have to walk all the way home alone on this important before-birthday afternoon of April the ninth, 1912. She forgot the sky and the things she always looked for like the Jones's bob-tail cat. Instead she stared down at the scuffed toes of her shoes. There had been sudden showers all day and now the delicate wings of the seeds from the maple trees were drifting down into the puddles on the pavement. She splashed through the water without stopping to think what Auntie Cris would say about wet feet. School was certainly better now, and that was good, but things at home were not better at all. They were much worse. She stooped to pick up one of the maple seedlings and flung it upwards to catch the breeze and fly away. No, things at home were not good at all.

Ever since the wonderful morning a week ago when her father had laughed and dropped his eggshell into Auntie Cris's coffee, he had been more and more sad. Then this morning he had told her that her mother was worse again and would have to have another operation. This was bad enough, but, on top of it, Helen was worried about her birthday. It began to look as though her father had forgotten all about it. He had not mentioned it once all the week and there had been no sign of a bicycle hidden away in the shed at the back of the garden, nor in the corner of the front porch behind the big table where she had discovered the Flexible Flyer sled that last Christmas before her mother was taken away to the hospital. Each morning, as Helen tied the ribbons on the end of her pigtails, she had decided that she would just mention the word *birthday* to her father. But when she had come down to the breakfast table to find him silent and busy with his paper, the word that she had practised saying so easily to her face in the mirror upstairs could not possibly be said downstairs in the silent dining-room. Several times she had tried, and had started to speak, only to have Auntie Cris clear her throat and rumble or tell her to 'run along now and get ready for school'.

It would be dreadful if everyone forgot about tomorrow being April the tenth. Perhaps when her father opened his paper the date at the top of the page would jump out at him. He would remember then, and laugh out loud, and give her twelve kisses and one extra large one to grow on. But then it would be too late to get the bicycle in time. It would have to be sent from Boston by train and then brought up from the station by Mr McGerrity's wagon and that always took a very long time. Everyone in Newton Lowlands said that Mr McGerrity *drank*, and everyone knew that he often left the freight piled up for days and days in the baggage room.

Of course, if the bicycle had been bought – if her father had remembered it after all – then she could, herself, ride it up from the station. Perhaps tonight, if her father didn't go to the hospital, he would come up to kiss her good night and then she could just casually suggest about riding the bicycle home. She had learned to ride on Barbara Buckingham's old one and she had been going to surprise her father by showing him how she could just get on and ride away but perhaps, since he seemed to have forgotten, it would be a good idea to tell him tonight. Perhaps she could remind Auntie Cris about Barbara Buckingham coming to supper, too. But that didn't matter so much because Barbara had already been asked. Still it would be awful if she came and there wasn't any place laid for her, or any special supper.

As Helen came around the corner into Hyde Street where she lived, she heard someone call her name. She stopped and looked up to see the Postman coming across the road towards her.

'You can save my old legs a few extra steps, Helen,' he said. 'I've only got one letter for the house at the end of the street and that is addressed to Miss Helen Hamilton. Know her?'

'Oh, yes. Oh, thanks, Mr Walsh.' Helen took the letter and turned it over in her hands. It was post-marked 'Boston' and was addressed in the familiar round writing that her father always used in his letters to her. She started to open it, and then stopped suddenly.

'What's the matter?' the old postman asked kindly. He had rested his leather bag on the hydrant and was waiting to hear her news. They had been friends as long as Helen could remember.

'I don't really know,' Helen said slowly. 'It's just that Daddy doesn't write me letters except when he goes away. I don't see why he should write me now when he's home. It's sort of strange, isn't it?'

'Haven't you got a birthday coming along? I seem to remember something about the month of April that's rather special.'

'Ye-es, but he's never written me before for my birthday.'

'Come along, open it up now, and stop worrying until you have something to worry about.'

Helen tore open the envelope and read the letter out loud slowly.

My dearest Nelly,
   You will be surprised to have a letter written from my office and I'm afraid you won't be very pleased to get it, but as you will be quite grown up tomorrow when you are twelve I know you will help me by being brave and patient. I have just learned that there is a doctor in New York who thinks he can get Mother really well and I must go off at once to see

him. I want him to do this operation and he is a very busy man. This means that I won't be home for your birthday supper party but I know Auntie Cris will do her best to give you and Barbara B. a good time.

And, my dear little Nell, the bicycle must wait, too. It isn't right to spend so much money for a toy when it ought to be used to get Mother well. You are big enough now to understand this. We will hope and pray that by next Christmas we shall be happy and together again and then, perhaps, we can celebrate with the presents you want most. For now I'm sending you a smaller gift and I think it will come tomorrow in Mr Walsh's mailbag. It is something I had when I was a boy and it meant a very great deal to me, so I hope it will to you, too.

Now I must run away to catch my train. Say a special birthday prayer for your mother and be my very dear twelve-year-old-grown-up daughter.

With much love,
from your devoted Father,

John Hamilton.

Helen found it very hard to read the last part of the letter. The words danced up and down on the page and her throat felt tight and sore. When she finally came to the end, she folded the paper neatly into its creases and put it back into the envelope. Then, with a great effort, she remembered how very old she was about to be. She looked up at Mr Walsh and even managed to smile.

'That's a good girl,' he said, putting a large heavy hand on her shoulder. 'Let me see that envelope. That letter was mailed in Boston at half past ten this morning and I'm delivering it in the afternoon mail. How's that for the U.S. Post Office, eh?'

'I guess it's good, but Boston's only eight miles from here and it only takes thirty-five minutes in the train.'

'Yes, but letters. Now that's a very different thing. But

what's more important just now is what it is that I'll be bringing you in my bag tomorrow.'

'I – I did want a bicycle very much, you see.'

'And you'll have it sure thing, come Christmas. And, in the meantime, there'll be this other present to get on with.'

'Yes.' Helen took back the letter and stuffed it into her pocket. Mr Walsh reached over to pick up his bag.

'If your mother gets well again and comes home, then that'll be the real birthday present to my way of thinking. And if you cheer up and help your father, you'll be getting that real present sure as fate.'

Helen thought about this for a minute and then she said slowly, 'Perhaps if I write Daddy a letter, that might be a good idea. I can send it to the office and he'll find it when he gets back from New York.'

Mr Walsh put down his bag again and felt in his trouser pocket. 'Look what I found,' he said, taking out a bright new coin. 'I was going to give you this on the right day but I might not get to your house before you go off to school and you'll want to buy a stamp for that letter, won't you?'

'Oh, yes – oh, thanks – that's wonderful.' Helen reached her arms as far as they would go around Mr Walsh's large middle and hugged him tightly. Then he stooped down to kiss the neat white parting on the top of her head, picked up his bag again and began to whistle.

'I do feel much better now,' Helen said.

'Well, you'd better run along or your auntie'll be calling the police out. And don't forget that one birthday's nothing in a lifetime. You wait till you get to be a hundred and one like me.'

This was an old joke and they laughed together. Then they both hurried off in opposite directions.

Helen went around to the back door where she was first

welcomed by Cindy, the cat, who rubbed his sunbaked fur against her legs and purred loudly. She was about to pick him up when she remembered that Auntie Cris didn't like to find black hairs on her school dress. She stooped down and patted him, putting her face near so that he could rub his cold nose against her cheek.

'I will invite you to my birthday party, in Daddy's place,' she told him, 'and if I have a birthday cake, I'll give you a large bite.'

But she did not wait to hear Cindy's answer. Her own words had reminded her of another worry. Suppose Auntie Cris didn't make a cake. Just suppose. What would Barbara Buckingham, who was so rich, think of a birthday party without a cake? Auntie Cris would remember if only she wasn't too busy. Surely with Father away, Auntie Cris wouldn't be quite so busy. But then she might just forget. And the worst of it was that you couldn't remind anyone about your own birthday cake.

Helen climbed the back steps slowly and went into the

kitchen. Auntie Cris was standing over the stove with her back to the door but she turned around as Helen came in.

'Your father's telephoned,' she said.

'Well, I know about his not being here on my birthday if that's what you were going to say.' Helen reached into her pocket. 'He sent me a letter.'

'Well, I never did. A letter. He's a very good father to you, Helen.'

For some reason, Helen did not want to be told that she had a very good father. It seemed so true that it spoiled it to say so out loud. It was almost a holy and unmentionable thing. She put her arithmetic book down on the checked red table cloth and said suddenly, 'Auntie Cris, I will have a birthday cake, won't I?'

'A birthday cake for only you two children! Goodness gracious me! Don't you think I have enough to do in this big house without making you a birthday cake? Now when I was your age – '

Helen didn't feel that she could bear to hear how good Auntie Cris had been when she was a little girl, and, without waiting to find out, she rushed through the kitchen and up the stairs to her own room at the top of the house.

There was a clean white counterpane on the bed and it looked frighteningly spick and span. Helen had been planning to throw herself down and have a good cry the way heroines did. In the best books they always said, 'After a good cry, she felt much better –' But in ordinary life there was always something like a clean bedspread that ought not to be creased. She stood quite still and looked around at all the familiar things in the room until she came to the ink spot on the wall, and that reminded her of the birthday when she had chosen the wallpaper with its silky grey stripes and its beautiful baskets of roses hung together with ribbon to make a border around the top. That was when she was seven. It was the kind of present her mother had always thought up – the kind you could choose yourself. That had been a wonderful birthday and no one had scolded her when she'd got the ink spot on the paper that night when she had tried writing poetry in bed. The next year she'd had the desk and the card had said, 'For writing poems, With love to Nelly from Mother and Father.' And the next year the carpet with more beautiful pink roses.

When she thought about these things, she didn't want to cry any more. Not many girls, except perhaps Susan, had rooms of their own with all their own things where they could come and be by themselves. Even Auntie Cris didn't often climb the stairs except on special cleaning days. As Helen went on looking around her, she began to feel more and more cheerful. Then she stopped staring and walked over to her desk by the window. The ink-well was dry but she found a pencil in the drawer and sat down. After chewing the end for a few moments, she wrote this letter:

Dearest Daddy,

I am not twelve yet and won't be until tomorrow but I am old enough at eleven years and 364 days to be able not to mind about the bicycle. So I hope you got the doctor all right.

Mr Walsh gave me your letter. He thinks the mail was very quick and we are both very interested in what he will bring me tomorrow.

Auntie Cris is busy in the kitchen but I think not making a cake. Well, I must close now. Cindy sends his love and I send mine plus kisses too,

from
Nelly.

P.S. Do you know if a guy can be a girl as well as a boy? I don't think so myself. This is very important so please remember to answer me whether I remember to ask you again or not.

As Helen folded the letter into an envelope she thought about this question which she had been meaning to ask her father for two days. If she was right, then Susan and Robert and all the others were wrong and she could make them look pretty silly, calling her a boy when she was a girl.

She got up and put the letter into the pocket of her school coat together with Mr Walsh's ten cent piece. She must leave a little early tomorrow morning in order to have time to stop at the Post Office on her way to school. As she hung the coat over the back of her chair, she fingered the coin in the pocket. There would be eight cents left for a large bag of sweets.

CHAPTER THREE

The Birthday

HELEN heard Auntie Cris calling her from a long way off. She opened one eye and then closed it again quickly. In the early morning, when Auntie Cris felt most stiff, she hated to climb the stairs and Helen's room at the top of the house was safe from attack. She decided to turn over and take one more small sleep. A ray of bright sunlight came slanting in through the window and fell on to the two tightly shut eyes. Helen blinked and then opened them both. There was some reason why, this morning, she must get up on time.

Of course. Birthday. April the tenth.

Helen was now wide awake. She slid out of bed and stood shivering by the window, looking into the top of the oak tree.

'Helen – oh, Helen – are you up?'

Helen opened the door, tiptoed out into the hall in her bare feet, and leaned over the banisters. 'Yes, Auntie, I'm up. And I'll be down in two minutes.'

A noise that might have been a cough, but might just possibly have been a laugh, came from the floor below. 'Mind you are, young lady. I've been calling off and on now for fifteen minutes.'

Helen hurried into her clothes. She had forgotten to hang up the checked gingham last night and now she smoothed down the creases anxiously. If only she could wear a clean dress every morning like Susan then she wouldn't need – ever – to hang anything up at night. But she didn't want to think about Susan. Everyone ought to feel new and different on a birthday. As she struggled with her plaits, she looked at her face in the mirror. It was exactly the same face. It didn't look newer, or happier, or prettier at all. It still had a small snub nose and what Auntie Cris called 'a sallow look'. Moreover, there was no sign of curl in the straight black hair except where the braids, when Helen undid them, made bands of crinkles, like Auntie's wash board.

Helen sighed as she snapped on the rubber bands, tied the red ribbons over them and combed out the stiff black tails at the end of each braid. Birthdays ought to make you over into all the things you wanted to be. But they never did. Perhaps next year when she was thirteen a sudden great change would come and she would find herself beautiful. Her mother would be at home then and when they walked together down the street, people would stop them and say, 'Why, Mrs Hamilton, is that Helen? But it *can't* be. I thought it must be your sister!' And then her mother would smile and say, 'Yes, Helen is in her teens now. She's changed a great deal.'

'*Helen Hamilton*, aren't you ever coming to your breakfast?'

Helen dropped the comb with a clatter and dashed headlong down the two steep flights of stairs to the kitchen. As she went in, there was a lovely smell of frying bacon and the back door was open so that she could see the sunlight in patches on the grass and beyond it the giant lilac bush with its bright new leaves and tight green buds. Cindy was meowing outside the screen door and Auntie Cris was singing *Bringing in the Sheaves*. The sounds were both good and, mixed up together, they made Helen want to laugh out loud.

She tiptoed across to the door and pushed it open quietly. Cindy walked in with an extra loud cry of greeting and rubbed against her legs. At the sound, Auntie Cris

30

turned around and stopped singing. Helen held her breath, waiting for her to say, 'Don't let that plaguy cat into this kitchen. One of these days I'll fall over him and break my neck – ' But she didn't say that at all. Instead, she smiled and looked down at Helen through her half-spectacles that made her eyes look so much larger than they really were, and said, 'Happy Birthday, Helen.'

Helen flung herself across the room. 'Mind my glasses,' Auntie Cris managed to say as Helen hugged her hard. Helen loved the starchy smell of the clean apron as she pressed her head against the bib part that covered Auntie's wide bosom. If birthdays didn't make you different yourself they did seem to make other people different, and that, she decided, could be even nicer.

'I thought, since your father was away, we'd have our breakfast out here and save my poor legs,' Auntie announced. 'You'd better sit down and start. School still keeps even if it is Miss Helen Hamilton's birthday.'

Helen saw that the table with the checked cloth under the kitchen window was laid for two and that there was a large box at her place.

'Oh, Auntie Cris – what's that?'

'Just something for a birthday girl,' Auntie said, looking very pleased.

'Can I open it first, or afterwards?'

'Better eat your breakfast. The present will keep, I shouldn't wonder.'

Helen helped herself to cornflakes and ate them very fast. In half a minute she announced that she was ready for her bacon.

'Well, I never did,' Auntie Cris said. She put a pile of thin bacon curls on to a plate with a piece of buttered toast. 'Pity we can't have presents every day.'

'Yes,' Helen agreed, 'a great pity. But I don't suppose you would want three hundred and sixty-five different things enough so that you'd eat up fast to get them every day. Perhaps, by the hundredth day, you'd say, "I don't believe I'll bother with my present this morning, I'll just wait until I have more time".' Helen put down her fork, held her hand over her mouth to make a yawn, and tried to look bored the way you might feel if you'd had a hundred presents.

'Well, that isn't very likely to happen,' Auntie Cris said practically, 'and now you just pick up that fork and get on with today's breakfast.'

Helen took up her fork but she was still thinking what it would be like to have a birthday every day. 'I suppose you could do it by saying, "I'm twelve years old plus one day," like a sum in arithmetic, "I'm twelve plus two days," and so on – . But I don't suppose it really would be much fun.'

'You are a case, Helen, and you do talk nonsense. Did you sleep in that dress last night?'

Helen had hoped the wrinkles wouldn't be noticed on a birthday. 'Not exactly,' she said and then filled her mouth with bacon and toast so that she wouldn't be expected to say any more.

'I see, I see – ' Auntie Cris didn't ever have any breakfast except coffee and now she sat back in her chair and her words turned into a little tune. 'I see, I see, said the blind man – and he couldn't see at all – at all – ' She's not going to scold me, then, Helen thought. Certainly this birthday had made Auntie into a very special person. How nice it would be if she would stay special for three hundred and sixty-five days.

'Well, are you going to sit there dreaming or are you going to open up your present?'

Helen started. 'Oh, my present – '

'Here, I'll clear away so you can open it out on the table.'

Helen undid the string, took off the cover, and folded back the tissue paper.

'Oh, Auntie,' she cried, 'it's a new dress – and it's pink and it's got embroidery on it.' She pulled it out of the box and held it up to her. 'Oh, Auntie, it's *heavenly*.'

'I don't know that it's all that beautiful, but it's nice and it has a good deep hem to it. And what a time I've had making it with you poking your nose into everything. I'd about given up trying to keep it a secret.'

'But you did, Auntie – you did. I never did see it until this minute. Oh – Can I put it on now, *please*? Can't I wear it to school? Just this once. Oh, please – you see – ' Helen stopped. She couldn't explain about Susan to anyone.

'No, I don't see any more than the blind man. I was going to say you could wear it tonight when Barbara comes to supper, but I suppose if you want to wear it all that much – '

Helen didn't wait to hear the end of the sentence. She took the new dress and, holding it carefully in front of her, rushed upstairs.

'How do I look?' she asked when, a few minutes later, she came back into the kitchen.

Auntie Cris turned around from the dishes in the sink and wiped her hands slowly on the roller towel. 'It does look good if I say so myself – the fit's real good, too,' she said slowly. Then she frowned suddenly, 'But you can't wear those red hair ribbons with a pink dress.'

'I – haven't got any pink ones.'

'What about those you had on last Sunday?'

'I lost one on the way home.'

She didn't want to explain, even now, how it happened. Robert Busby had been hiding behind the syringa bush by the railway station. He'd jumped out as she came by and snatched it off. And all the week long he'd been keeping it in his desk at school and showing it to everyone. Once he'd even tied it on the big red lock of his own hair that hung down into his eyes. Then he'd danced around the playground at break and called himself 'The Funny Guy'. Helen couldn't bear to think about it, so she said quickly, 'I don't mind these. There's a reddy bit in the embroidery anyway.'

'Well – But what will you do come Sunday?'

34

'It doesn't matter.' Helen wanted to go now. She didn't want to think about anything except the new dress.

'Well, get your coat, then.'

'Must I?'

'Yes, of course you must. April's treacherous weather. What a silly child you are.'

Helen suddenly remembered the letter and the money and went to get her coat quite cheerfully. When she came back Auntie Cris was fumbling in her old black handbag. She brought out a twenty-five cent piece and handed it to Helen. 'Stop at Belcher's on your way home from school. You'd better get two yards while you're about it, and mind you get the right shade of pink.'

'Oh, thanks – thanks ever so much.' Helen was about to try another hug when she remembered that she had on the new dress. Then to her surprise, Auntie Cris bent over and held her soft cheek to be kissed.

Yes, Helen thought, as she practised her skipping steps down Hyde Street, so far it had been a perfect day – that is – as perfect a day as she could possibly have without either a mother or a father at home. She'd never known Auntie Cris to be so nice, and it was a lovely partyish kind of dress – perhaps not quite so party as Susan's but not a bit like her own ordinary everyday dresses.

Now if only the rest of the day would go on being good she would remember this birthday all the days of her life. She passed the station and saw old Mr McGerrity nodding on the seat of his wagon. She was hurrying along Main Street when she suddenly thought that if she bought the pink ribbons on the way to school, she could put them on in the dressing-room and everything would be quite perfect. She could just see the clock on the church tower from the front of Belcher's, and it said twenty-five minutes past eight. That ought to be plenty of time.

But when she got inside, Mrs Belcher was busy selling

sweets and that reminded Helen that she had been meaning to buy some with the rest of Mr Walsh's ten cents. It
also reminded her that she had to stop at the Post Office to
buy the stamp for her father's letter. Perhaps she ought not
to wait. But it would be wonderful to have her ribbons
match. She looked at the big wooden rack with rolls and
rolls of ribbon, lovely satiny pinks, and blues and yellows
and greens.

'What can I do for you, young lady?'

Helen jumped, and then looked up eagerly. Mrs Belcher helped her match the colour and cut the ribbon
neatly into four half-yard lengths.

'It's my birthday,' Helen explained as she took the
screwed up paper parcel. 'That's why I'm having new
ribbons to match my new dress.'

'I see.' Mrs Belcher walked along to the sweet counter
and reached inside the glass case. 'Better have a Tootsie
Roll for break then.'

Helen was so surprised that she almost forgot to thank
Mrs Belcher. She put the lovely chewy chocolate in her
pocket and hurried out into the street. But now she could
see quite plainly that the clock in the church tower said
twenty-eight minutes to nine.

She was late already. She flew down the road, her heart
beating wildly. Suddenly everything seemed to have gone
wrong. She *should* have bought the stamp and mailed the
letter. She *shouldn't* have bought hair ribbons until after
school. And now she wouldn't have time to tie them on
anyway. When she reached the school building, the bell
had stopped ringing, and the outside door was shut. She
tugged it open and hurried into the dressing-room to take
off her coat and hang it on the hook. She could hear a
murmur of voices in the schoolroom. They were saluting
the flag. She couldn't go in now. Perhaps, since she was
late anyway, it wouldn't hurt to be a little later. She un-

36

twisted the screw of paper and went to the mirror. But just as she was admiring the first pink bow, so perfectly matching the pink dress, the door behind her opened suddenly and Helen could see in the mirror that it was Susan Johnson who peered around it.

'Teacher says she heard you, and you're late, and you're to come in at once.' Susan made this announcement with great pleasure.

Helen forgot everything except that she hated Susan Johnson and that she was late. She walked slowly into the room that seemed to be full of staring faces and went to her seat. Anyway, they would all see the new dress. They would all see that Helen Hamilton looked better than any other girl in the class.

'What happened to you, Helen?' Miss Perkins asked.

Everyone would tease her at break if she told about the hair ribbons. She thought quickly and then said, 'Well, you see, just as I came by the station, Mr McGerrity's horse started up. And he ran and he ran and he ran. Mr McGerrity was asleep but he woke up and fell off. He was a little hurt and I stopped to help him up and then we both chased after the horse. But he went on, and on, and on – '

Someone laughed, and Helen stopped suddenly.

'Come up to the desk, Helen,' Miss Perkins said quietly.

Helen struggled to her feet and walked slowly up the aisle. She could feel the hot blush in her cheeks and even behind her ears. When she came near to the desk she stopped and stared down at the toes of her shoes.

'Do you think Mr McGerrity's horse was frightened at seeing a girl with one red hair ribbon and one pink one?' Miss Perkins asked.

Now every boy and girl in the room laughed except Helen who didn't feel like laughing at all. She reached up

37

and pulled off the red ribbon and stuffed it into her pocket.

'You can stay after school this afternoon and write me a story about Mr McGerrity's horse, and now you can go back to your seat.'

Even Miss Perkins seemed to be laughing, and to make it worse, as Helen walked back down the aisle she could hear someone whisper, 'The Funny Guy – The Funny Guy – '

But, after the bad beginning, the rest of the day at school went better. Betty Higgins, who was Susan Johnson's best friend, told Helen at break that she thought her new dress was lovely and then helped her to tie on the other pink ribbon. After that they took turns with bites of Helen's Tootsie Roll. And, on the way home, at mid-day, she remembered to buy the stamp and mail the letter to her father, and to get a striped bag of sweets with some of the left-over pennies.

At lunch, there were two more parcels at Helen's place and Auntie Cris was still cheerful and still singing, 'I see, I see said the blind man – ' But she stopped long enough to say, 'Mr Walsh brought these just after you left this morning. He said he hurried a-purpose but he must have just missed you. Perhaps it's as well. You might have been late for school.'

Helen started to say, 'I was late anyway,' and then thought better of it. Instead, she said, 'Yes. Anyway, it's more fun to open them now when I don't have to hurry.'

It was quite easy to see that one parcel was a rolled-up magazine. Helen opened that first and flattened it out on the table. 'ST NICHOLAS'. She read out the words, and then said quickly, 'Some of the children at school have this. It has some good stories in it.' She turned the pages slowly and, when a slip of paper fell out, she picked it up and tried not to let Auntie Cris know how she was feeling. Just an old magazine. The paper said, 'St Nicholas Magazine will come to Helen Hamilton every month from April 1912 to April 1913 as a present from her loving father.' The words 'Helen Hamilton', 'April 1912', 'April 1913' and 'her loving father' had been written in, but the rest was a printed card with fancy lettering and a fancy border of scrolls and ribbons around the edge. This, then, was the present her father had written about. This magazine must have been what he liked when he was a boy. But it didn't seem like a real present. It wasn't anything like a bicycle.

'For goodness' sakes, what's the matter, Helen? You are a funny child and no mistake.'

'Nothing's the matter,' Helen said quickly. 'I just haven't got used to this yet. I never had a magazine before, did I?'

'Well, what's in the other parcel?' Auntie Cris said. 'It's postmarked "Boston". Now who else do you know in Boston?'

Helen had forgotten about the other parcel and she turned to it eagerly. Inside the brown paper wrapping was a square box and a letter. 'I'll read this first,' she decided. The writing was very grown up and difficult but she managed to spell it out slowly:

Dear Helen,

A few months ago when your mother was so much better, she wrote a letter and ordered this for your birthday on April the 10th. I hope I have remembered the date right and that you have many happy returns of the day –

Sincerely yours,
Nurse Brandon.

'Why, that's the nurse in the hospital,' Helen said. 'She's nice and has red hair, not carroty like Robert Busby's but dark and – and rich.'

'Well, open up the box and let's see what's inside. You haven't got all day. School keeps this afternoon, same as usual.'

'Yes, I know.' But Helen held the box in her hand without moving. She was thinking about the letter and how it said, 'a few months ago when your mother was better' – and now she must be worse or she would have sent the parcel herself and written her own letter. Maybe she was much worse. A tear splashed down on to the box and made a round dark stain on the shining surface. Helen wiped it away quickly, took off the cover and looked across the table at Auntie Cris.

'Oh – it's most lovely pink writing paper with envelopes,' she said. 'And it's got a monogram on it – a real monogram, look – ' Helen handed the box across the table, and went to stand behind Auntie Cris's chair. Two beautiful curlycue H's stood side by side with the middle upright line belonging to both letters and the cross line running through them both. It was printed in pure gold.

'Well, I never did,' Auntie Cris said.

'The first letter I write will be to Mother,' Helen said. But she didn't say that she had already decided to take the box to school because she was afraid Auntie Cris wouldn't let her – and she had to. Maybe she could write the letter there if she got her geography done as quickly as she usually did. Besides, she wanted to show this special present to Miss Perkins, and she would have time after school since she had to stay anyway and write about Mr McGerrity's horse.

All the way to school Helen thought about her mother. She was probably lying in the high hospital bed with the shade drawn and all the magazines and books untouched on the table. Would she ever get up and be gay the way she used to be? Or would she just get weaker and weaker until – No, Helen couldn't even think the ugly word.

Surely the new doctor would make her mother well again.

It was just two years ago that the message had come to school. Miss Sampson had been Helen's teacher and everything had been all right. She hadn't been a funny guy then. She had been just ordinary like everyone else, even Susan Johnson and Robert Busby. Miss Sampson had called her up to the desk and asked her to come out into the hall. Then together they had gone to Mr Miller's office. She could feel Miss Sampson's soft light hand on her shoulder and hear Mr Miller say, 'I've just had a message from your father, Helen. Your mother was crossing Tremont Street in Boston when a runaway horse came charging down Park Street. I'm afraid she's been run over – but she isn't seriously hurt.' He had said these last words quickly and as Helen remembered them now she thought he had spoken them too quickly because he didn't quite believe them himself.

'Sit down, Helen,' Miss Sampson had said, and her voice had sounded very far away.

Helen remembered sitting down and being given something to smell. When she could listen again, Mr Miller went on. 'You're to go home to your friend's house. Let me see, I've written down the name – Barbara Buckingham, is it?'

'Yes,' Helen heard herself say faintly, and then, 'She goes to a private school in Brookline.'

'Well, she'll be home earlier than you then.' He got up and came to stand near Helen. 'I'm sure your mother'll be all right, Helen. It's just a few broken bones and your father says they didn't waste any time getting her into the hospital.'

Yes, that had all happened two years ago. Since then

her mother had never left the hospital, not once, and sometimes Helen couldn't even go to see her for months and months.

That night after Helen had gone to bed, she lay awake for a long time thinking about all the things that had happened during the day.

She was very glad she had taken the writing paper to school that afternoon, because, when Miss Perkins discovered that it was a birthday present, she hadn't made Helen stay and write the story about Mr McGerrity after all. Instead, she had talked to her about telling the truth. Helen had tried to explain that sometimes the untruth seemed to pop out first and she just couldn't help it. But Miss Perkins couldn't understand that at all.

Perhaps Helen really was different from every other girl and boy in the world. Perhaps something strange and awful had happened to her at the very moment that the accident had happened to her mother.

Well, anyway, there *had* been a birthday cake. Auntie Cris had made it, too, with icing and candles on it. Barbara Buckingham had given Helen a game of Parcheesi which was fun to play because they had tried it out after supper. If only there was someone else besides Barbara to play it with, though. Barbara wasn't really much use. She kept saying, 'I do like this game I gave you, don't you?' And finally when Helen got tired of saying 'Yes', and said 'No', and shoved the board over so the round counters danced out of their places, Barbara began to cry like a baby and said she wanted to go home.

That was the trouble with Barbara. She was always like that. Of course she was pretty with long curls like Susan's only not quite so golden, and she was nearly a year younger than Helen and went to a private school. What was more she was spoilt and had what Helen's father had once called 'a sheltered life'. It was true that Barbara's mother never would let her do exciting things. She couldn't even ride her bicycle except around the block. But then Barbara never wanted to much because she was scared to cross the road. It was a great pity. Still, Helen had lived with the Buckinghams for a while until Auntie Cris had come. And now that Helen had turned into The Funny Guy at school, Barbara was her only real friend, and true friendship was a serious thing. You had to put up with a great deal for the sake of friendship.

Just as Helen was thinking these thoughts and dropping off to sleep, she remembered that she hadn't said her prayers, so she climbed out and knelt beside the bed. The floor felt cold under her knees but she said the long prayer with the special part for her mother to get better that she always put on at the end.

At last she got back into bed and thought about her mother and the wonderful pink writing paper. Then, when she was almost asleep, she remembered her *St Nicholas*. She hadn't even looked at it since lunch. Well, she would tomorrow. She would read it straight through from cover to cover.

CHAPTER FOUR

Trouble with St Nicholas

On the morning after her birthday, Helen again put on her new dress and went downstairs to find Auntie Cris in the kitchen. The table was set for two and there was the same good smell of bacon and toast but Helen knew at once, when she saw Auntie Cris's back, that it wasn't going to be like the birthday morning in any other way. She slid into her seat quietly and waited.

Presently Auntie Cris turned from the stove and, seeing Helen, gave a sudden start. 'Goodness gracious, how you frightened me, sitting there all the time and I never knew it,' she said. 'I very nearly dropped the plate.' Her round face had the pinched tired look that Helen had come to know very well. It meant that Auntie Cris's rheumatism was worse and that Helen must be especially careful what she said.

'I go creeping about like a mouse, don't I?' she remarked cheerfully.

'A much too fancy mouse, I'd say, by the look of you.' Auntie Cris's eyes, over the top of her half-glasses, were very fierce. 'Whatever possessed you to put that dress on again today?'

'Oh, please, Auntie Cris – it's so beautiful and I do love it so much.'

'It won't be beautiful long, young lady, if you wear it to school every day in the week.' Auntie Cris let herself down heavily into the rocker by the window. 'Plague take it, I've left my cup on the back of the stove and I do want my coffee if I don't want anything else,' she added.

Helen got up quickly. 'I'll get it for you,' she said.

In three running steps Helen had crossed the kitchen but she was so intent on getting to the stove before Auntie Cris stopped her, that she didn't see Cindy yawn, stretch and come towards her from his basket by the stove. Helen reached for the cup and stumbled over Cindy at the same moment. There was a clatter, a frightened 'meow', a crash, and then a dreadful silence.

As Cindy fled back to his basket in terror, Helen stood still and looked down, first at the broken cup on the floor, and then at the ugly stain running like a dark brown river from neck to hem of her new pink dress.

'Oh,' she said in a frightened voice. And then again, 'Oh.'

Auntie Cris got up painfully from her chair. 'Pride goes before a fall,' she said and her voice sounded far away and angry. 'What was I just telling you about wearing that dress? Just look at yourself now.'

Helen said nothing. Why did everything have to go wrong all at once? She looked up at Auntie Cris and then down at her dress and the puddle of coffee and bits of broken china on the floor.

'Well,' Auntie Cris went on, and Helen noticed that she sounded a little less fierce. 'There's no good crying over spilt coffee. You go up and change your dress. I'll clean up this mess. And when you come down you're to put that plaguy cat outdoors where he belongs.'

'Oh, Auntie, will it come out, do you think?'

'That stain on your dress? I expect so, if I tend to it right away. Bring it down with you and I'll see to it.'

Helen climbed the stairs to her room. Then, slowly, she changed back into the wrinkled gingham. If she could keep looking round the familiar room at her own precious things, it helped to keep back the tears. There was the wallpaper with its ink spot, the clean white bedspread, her

45

desk by the window. And there, on the desk, lay her copy of *St Nicholas Magazine*, still curled up from its wrapping. Lying there, it was like a good omen. It seemed to be reminding her of her father and how he had said he liked it when he was her age. Perhaps it would be a comforter for this day that had started all wrong. She picked up the little bundle of her coffee-stained dress from the floor where she had stepped out of it and reached for *St Nicholas* with her other hand. Perhaps there would be time to read it during break, or even behind the cover of her desk, if only Miss Perkins would be busy enough not to notice.

When Helen started off to school half an hour later, Cindy followed her down the path and then climbed up on the gate post to finish washing the coffee off his neat black coat. Helen stood for a moment to watch his small pink tongue hard at work and thought how much easier spills were for cats than for humans. Then she pushed her arithmetic book and *St Nicholas* tighter under her arm and went off down the road. Cindy stopped to watch the departure of his mistress, but when she looked back, he had returned to the serious business of washing.

At half past eleven Miss Perkins divided the class into two for the geography lesson. While the first half were reciting, the others were expected to start on their homework. This was the opportunity Helen had been waiting for. She lifted her desk cover quietly and reached for her largest book, *The Geography of North America.* Then she worked her hands busily inside the desk for a few moments before she put down the lid, opened the heavy volume, and began to turn the pages. No one except Susan Johnson noticed that Helen was reading a story called *The Lucky Sixpence* in a magazine called *St Nicholas*, and that it had nothing whatever to do with the lakes and rivers of Canada.

46

Although the story was a serial and had started a few months ago, Helen soon became so absorbed in it that she did not notice the unusual activity behind her. Susan waited until Miss Perkins was very busy on the other side of the room and then slid a note across to Robert Busby. He read it under his desk cover and made a signal in answer. A moment later he got up and walked up the aisle to get a piece of clean paper from the pile on Miss Perkins's desk. All his movements were very slow and, as he turned to go back to his seat, Miss Perkins put down the pointer she had been using on the wall map and watched him.

Helen did not see or hear anything that was happening in the room. The big geography had worked its way out from under the magazine and now stuck out over the edge of the desk. As Robert passed down the aisle, his long arm swooped down suddenly and gave the heavy book a sudden shove. It slid with a loud clatter to the floor, leaving *St Nicholas Magazine* alone and in full view on Helen's desk.

Helen did not dare to look up. Brisk steps could be heard crossing the room and, before Robert, with a great deal of fuss, could pick up the geography from the floor or Helen could hide the magazine, Miss Perkins was standing over them both.

There was a moment of silence and then, 'You are unusually clumsy today, aren't you, Robert,' Miss Perkins asked quietly.

Robert mumbled an answer, put the geography on Helen's desk, and shambled back to his seat.

Miss Perkins looked down at the magazine open in front of Helen. 'Is that part of your homework?' she asked pleasantly.

Helen felt her cheeks burn hotly and she couldn't look up as she managed to whisper, 'No, Miss Perkins.'

'I'll take the magazine then, I think,' Miss Perkins said.

Helen clutched it suddenly with both hands. 'No. Oh, please, no. I have to have it. You see, my father –' Her voice trailed off helplessly.

'All the same I think I'll take charge of it for the present and' – she turned suddenly to Robert who, in the safety of his seat, was grinning happily at Susan – 'Robert, bring me that paper on the floor under your desk.'

Robert stopped looking at Susan and the Cheshire Cat

smile disappeared from his face as he reached down for the telltale note. When Miss Perkins had read it, she said quietly, 'I'd like to have Robert and Susan and Helen stay on for a little while after school. I think we have a few things to say to each other.'

She took the copy of *St Nicholas* to her desk and then went back to the wall map. In a moment her pointer was as busy as if nothing whatever had happened.

For Helen, the rest of the long day dragged wearily by. At lunchtime Auntie Cris was silent and Helen didn't even dare to ask her if the coffee stain had come out of the new dress. She ate her lunch quickly and went out in the garden to talk things over with Cindy but there was no small black ball curled up on the fence post, or under the lilac bush, or in any of his favourite places. Helen decided that he must be off on one of his trips of adventure but she was very disappointed in him for choosing this day when she needed him so much.

It was too early to start back to school so she went in and dried the lunch dishes for Auntie Cris who was still silent and busy with her own thoughts. Helen wondered if Auntie was thinking about her son who had been a sailor and whose photograph stood on her chest of drawers. He had run away to sea and had never come back but he'd sent that photograph from Jamaica in the West Indies. He looked like Auntie Cris except that he was thin and young and a man. In a corner in faded ink you could just read the words, 'Love to Ma from Johnny.'

As she watched Auntie Cris washing the dishes with her lips buttoned tight over each other, Helen couldn't help thinking about Auntie's lost only son. It always made Helen feel sad to think about him and, all at once, she had to say something out loud to take away the sadness.

'Auntie,' she said, and her words stumbled over each other because she was a little frightened to be saying them at all, 'I do think Johnny will come back some day. I – I feel it in my bones.'

'What's that you're saying, child?'

'Only that I feel it in my bones that Johnny is going to come back some day.'

'Your bones aren't old enough to feel anything – let alone such nonsense.'

'It isn't nonsense, Auntie. And I do feel it in my bones.'

'Don't go filling your head with worrying about my Johnny, Helen. If the good Lord intends it, he'll come back. And if He doesn't, then He knows best.'

Helen didn't like it when Auntie stopped a conversation by bringing in the good Lord. Besides, Helen did have a feeling that Johnny would come back. Sometimes before she went to sleep at night she would see the man in the faded picture, only much older, even older than Daddy, come up the front steps and say, 'Hello, Ma, I'm Johnny.' But it wasn't any use trying to make Auntie understand this. Helen sighed as she wiped the last dish in the rack and went to hang up the towel.

And then she had to say just one more thing about Johnny. It was something that had been worrying her for a long time. 'Suppose –' she said slowly, turning around without hanging up the dish towel.

'Suppose what?' Auntie said in the voice she used when she wasn't really listening.

'Oh, do listen, *please*, Auntie. It's important. Suppose Johnny did write you a letter after all these years. How would you ever get it?'

'Well, he won't write me. That's certain sure. He wasn't much of a one for writing letters.'

'I know, but just suppose he did, or someone did for him – then what?'

'Well now, let me see. I reckon he'd write to Brighton

where we were living when he ran off. Then the Post Office would forward it to Islington and Mrs Barnes would send it on to Mrs Prouty's where I boarded when I was a seamstress. And Mrs Prouty – '

'Yes, what about Mrs Prouty?'

'Oh, you and your everlasting questions. I suppose she'd send it on to Mrs Ginty's where I live now – that is when I'm not living here.'

'But you're not *sure* about Mrs Prouty, are you?' And when Auntie Cris didn't answer, Helen persisted, 'Are you, Auntie?'

'Oh, do stop your pestering, Helen. My Johnny isn't going to write to his old ma after all these years. He'd think me dead and gone; if he ain't dead and gone himself.'

Helen knew that when Auntie said 'ain't' it meant that she was worried or distracted. Helen decided to make her point quite clear. 'Well, I know that a chain is as strong as the weakest link, and that's an awful long chain of people, Auntie Cris.'

'Wherever did you pick up that old saying?' Auntie Cris asked, and then, when Helen didn't answer, she went on, 'You're a good girl, Nelly, even if you are a queer one.'

'Oh, I'm *not* queer.' Helen couldn't bear to have Auntie Cris think she was a funny guy, too.

But Auntie was too tired to bother any more. She sank heavily into her chair by the window. 'You run along to school now, queer or not queer, and let me rest in peace.'

The afternoon at school was no better than the morning had been, and by half past three Helen was certain that Miss Perkins would never let her have her *St Nicholas* again. She kept wondering how she would ever be able to tell her father what had happened. As the others filed out behind Miss Perkins, Robert and Susan and Helen sat on in their seats.

Helen took out her homework but Susan whispered across to Robert, 'What note was it?'

'Yours,' Robert answered and then added, 'Shsh,' as Miss Perkins came back into the room. She went directly to her desk, sat down and, without looking at the children, became very busy. Perhaps she was correcting papers. It was evident that she did not want to be aware that there was anyone else in the room.

It was almost half an hour later when Miss Perkins finally put aside her pencil and walked down the aisle to stand near the three children. Then she said slowly, 'Susan, your note to Robert was very mysterious to me. Who is this "Funny Guy"?'

Susan stood up and her curls bobbed as she answered, in the special teacher voice that Helen hated, 'It's just a name, Miss Perkins,' she said.

'Just a name? This note from "Sue" is yours, isn't it?'

After a moment Susan said, 'Yes'.

'Well, perhaps you've forgotten what it said so I'll read it to you: "Dear Bob, The Funny Guy is reading a magazine inside her geography. I can see from here. Can't you do something?" – and it's signed "Love, Sue".'

Helen looked across at Susan. The clock over the blackboard ticked loudly in the silence and Helen felt her heart beating with it. Would Susan tell Miss Perkins the truth about the name? Helen crossed her feet under the table and her hands in her lap and repeated to herself, 'No, she mustn't. She mustn't. No, she mustn't, until it became a chant inside her head.

Robert Busby put up his hand and Miss Perkins turned to him. 'Well, Robert, what have you got to say about all this?'

Robert jumped to his feet and his words came quickly – the awful words that Helen had been dreading.

'We all call Helen "The Funny Guy". It's just a sort of a joke really. She's always doing such funny things like, well, like going on saluting the flag when everyone else's finished, and all that crazy story about Mr McGerrity's horse running away –'

'I see. So you and Susan and the others like to stick in pins to see if you can make her funnier, don't you?'

'Stick in pins?' Robert asked stupidly.

'I mean you all tease and torment, don't you?'

'Well, she's – '

'I see. How long has this been going on?'

'For ages,' Susan contributed and, warming to her subject, she went on eagerly, 'You see, it all started with a dare.'

'Perhaps Helen will tell me about it,' Miss Perkins said quietly.

Three pairs of eyes looked at Helen, and Helen looked down at the sums she had been doing on the smudgy yellow paper on her desk. She couldn't look up but she could feel the eyes that seemed to be closing in – closer and closer on every side.

'Please,' she heard herself say. 'I'd rather not talk about it. It doesn't matter now. I don't mind being called – anything – it's just like a nickname now – '

She stopped speaking and then from far away she heard Miss Perkins say, 'You're quite right, Helen, nicknames don't matter if we don't mind them.' She walked up to her desk and came back with Helen's *St Nicholas*. 'I've been having a look at this since I confiscated it. You ought to join the *St Nicholas League*, Helen. I believe you might win all kinds of honours and make us all proud of you.'

Helen took the magazine and tried to say, 'Thank you,'

but the words came out like a queer strangled noise. At any rate she could look up now. Miss Perkins was smiling and Helen forgot Robert and Susan and all the troubles of her life. She felt happier than she had felt for a very long time.

'You can all go now,' Miss Perkins said crisply, 'and in future, Susan and Robert and Helen, I want you to remember that a classroom, like a ship, has *one* captain.'

CHAPTER FIVE

Fun with St Nicholas

HAD Miss Perkins been serious, Helen wondered as she turned the pages of *St Nicholas* headed *St Nicholas League*? It would be quite easy for Helen to join, she learned, since anyone could be a member until they were eighteen, and all you had to do, was to draw a picture, write a verse, story, or essay, send in a photograph, or make up a puzzle. It was a rainy afternoon and Helen had nothing else to do, so she sat down at her desk and wrote a poem for a subject given, which was 'In Meadows Green'. It didn't take long and, at first, Helen thought it was quite the best poem that anyone had ever written. But, after she had read it over three times, she decided that it wasn't even good enough to send in.

The next day she thought she would try a story about 'An Unusual Experience' which was one of the subjects suggested. The trouble was that there were so many experiences. What could possibly make one of them more *unusual* than the others? She didn't want to write about her own worst experience but perhaps that really was unusual. Perhaps she *had* to write it, like a sort of punishment because she hadn't wanted to tell Miss Perkins, or anyone, about it. For two days she worried over this and then she decided to write it as if it were an unusual experience that had happened to someone else. This made it much easier – almost too easy – because, when she began to write, she wanted to say it in many more words than three hundred, and the rules said she mustn't write more. It took her two afternoons and a Saturday and Sunday to get the story finished, but it looked very neat when she had copied it out. She held it flat on her desk and read it over one last time.

An Unusual Experience

One warm day of early summer, Mary Parks was going to school. She hadn't been very happy for a long time because her mother had been sick and she had troubles at home and at school. But this was an especially nice morning so she took the long way around by the wood road to look for violets. But she hadn't gone far when she met a whole crowd of boys and girls from her grade and she was frightened. Lately they had teased her a lot because, thinking about her troubles, she had done silly things that made them laugh. She tried to take a side path through the woods before they saw her but one of the boys called William, who was her worst enemy, saw her and a minute later she was surrounded.

'Mary, Mary, quite contrary – ' they sang and said together, and then William held out a small green leaf with an extra large inch-worm arching his back in the middle of it.

'Bet you don't dare to touch it,' Jane said. She was another enemy but she was pretty with long golden curls and Mary was quite the opposite.

Mary reached out her finger and touched the worm. It felt soft. She didn't mind in the least.

Then William said, 'Bet you don't dare to eat it.'

Mary looked at the worm. He wasn't very large really and the leaf he was on was sorrel and Mary liked to eat sorrel very much. She looked at all the boys and girls looking at her and she thought that if she did this brave act, they would think she was wonderful. So, before she could think too much, she snatched the leaf, rolled the worm up in it, and ate him. He tasted just like sorrel.

Then all the boys and girls just stared at her. They stared and stared. They didn't think she was wonderful at all, or even brave.

Jane said, 'You're a Funny Guy, that's what you are.'

And then all the others called out, 'Funny Guy – Funny Guy,' and ran away so that Mary had to go to school by herself.

But she didn't mind too much because she had had an unusual experience.

After Helen had read her story through, she counted the words and found that it was still too long. Then she read the rules again to see if the League didn't allow more words for special entries or for any other reason. There was nothing about more words at all, but there was something worse. The closing date was April the 10th! She looked at her calendar. April 19th. She was much too late. Counting the days backwards on her fingers, she discovered that it had been too late even when the magazine first came. Yes, of course, that was right because the 10th was her birthday.

Helen put the story away carefully in the drawer of her desk. It did seem a great pity that it had to be wasted. And how could anyone ever send anything in to the League if the closing date came before the magazine did?

The next morning at breakfast, Helen decided to discuss this problem with her father. When he had read the most important parts of the newspaper and had put it down to stir his coffee, he smiled at her.

'Did you ever belong to *St Nicholas League*, Daddy?' she asked.

'Oh, yes, indeed I did. But the first thing I sent in I wrote in pencil so I got listed in "The Roll of the Careless". After that I did better and I got a badge or something, I seem to remember.'

'Was it gold or silver?' Helen asked anxiously.

'I haven't an idea – or whatever became of it.' Then, seeing Helen's look of disappointment, he added, 'You'll have to get one for yourself and find out.'

'Yes. Well, I did a first try but I can't send it in because it's April the 20th today and it had to be in by the 10th. What am I ever going to do? I didn't even get the magazine until the closing day.'

'Oh, that's easily explained. They sent you the April number because I ordered it for your birthday, but usually the April magazine comes in March so you would have had plenty of time. Any day now, you'll be getting the May number.'

'Well, I don't see how I can use what I've written then because there won't be the same subject. I wrote about *"An Unusual Experience"*.'

'Better let me have a look at it. Perhaps we can change the title. Anyway, I think I have to sign that it's an original work, don't I?'

This was exactly what Helen had been wanting her father to say but now that he had said it, she discovered that she didn't want him to read about Mary's unusual experience. She stared down into her milk, and then drank it slowly. As she hoped, her father's eye had been caught by a headline he had missed and he didn't repeat the question. Then Auntie Cris bustled in with a plate of toast and told Helen to get on with her milk or she'd be late.

That afternoon, on her way home from school, Helen met Mr Walsh, the Postman, and found that he had the May number of *St Nicholas* for her. Her father had been right, as he always was. She was very anxious to get home and see what the subjects for the new contest were, but when Mr Walsh took off his mail bag and set it against the hydrant, she knew that he wanted to have what he called 'a nice little chat' with her.

'How's your mother?' he began.

Helen hadn't wanted him to ask this question. She never wanted anyone, even Miss Perkins, to ask about her mother. If only she could just say, 'Very well, thank you,' without thinking, the way everyone else did, or even, 'On the mend,' it would be different. She began to tear at the brown paper wrapping of her magazine.

'My father's got a new doctor who has high hopes,' she said slowly. Then a lump came into her throat, as it always did, but she managed to say, 'She's to have another operation. He thinks it isn't only the leg that got broken but something else – something inside her – '

Seeing Helen's distress, Mr Walsh changed the subject quickly. 'Why do your friends call you "The Funny Guy"? Seems a crazy name for a girl, don't it?'

'Yes. Well, it is – crazy, I mean. But it's just a sort of nickname.' So Mr Walsh had heard, too. 'It's crazy because my father says a guy can't be a girl,' she went on quickly. 'He says in England a man called Guy Fawkes (his real name was Guido but they called him Guy) had a plot to blow up the Government, or anyway the buildings where the Government was, but he was caught before he did, so ever since then, they've been having a sort of Fourth of July kind of day on the Fifth of November when the plot was. They make stuffed scarecrows out of any old junk and set them on fire, and they call it burning the "guy".'

'Do tell. I never did hear the like of that before. Well, now, a real nice girl like you couldn't be a guy then, could she?'

'No.' Helen did like to hear Mr Walsh call her 'real nice'. She felt much better now. 'That's what I said to Robert Busby but he only laughed. He thinks he's very funny but he's a great guy himself.'

Mr Walsh picked up his bag and hung it on his shoulder. 'Well, we'll get rid of him next Fifth of November, shall we?'

'It's a long way ahead.' Helen laughed, thinking what

fun it would be to give Robert and Susan, and all of them, a good scare.

'It takes a long time to hatch a plot,' Mr Walsh whispered before he went off down the road.

Helen knew that he would turn and wave when he came to the corner so she waited impatiently. At last he had waved and gone and she could dash home. There she found Auntie Cris in the kitchen. She was sitting in her rocker shelling peas and Helen, fearing the worst, said a short quick, 'Hello, Auntie,' and made for the stairs to her room.

But it was no use. Auntie Cris called her back. As Helen shelled the peas into the large brown bowl in Auntie's lap, she thought how nice it would be to be rich like Barbara Buckingham who had probably never shelled so much as a pea in her life. But Auntie Cris's rheumatism was better and she sang all the hymns Helen liked best: *Rock of Ages, Oh Master Let Me Walk with Thee*, and even *Onward Christian Soldiers* which Auntie Cris didn't really approve of. She always said there was enough trouble in the world without Christians fighting.

When Auntie stopped to catch her breath, Helen said quickly, 'I didn't know you could get peas until the Fourth of July.'

'I didn't know it myself and that's a fact. But Mr Damiano down at the fruit and vegetable store says these peas come all the way from California,' Auntie announced.

'California,' Helen said, 'but that's thousands of miles away. They must be awful old peas.'

'Not a bit of it. Come in a refrigerator car – they call it – all packed up in ice.'

Helen looked at the peas in her hand. Somehow they seemed much more important having travelled all that distance. But a moment later she had forgotten about the peas, and she said suddenly, 'When you sang in the choir

in your church did they pay you much money for it?'

'Not enough to keep body and soul together,' Auntie said sadly. 'I often think my boy wouldn't have run away to sea if I'd been able to give him more comforts at home.'

'Didn't you have a husband?' This was a question Helen had been wanting to ask for a long time but no moment had seemed quite right for it. Even now she held her breath for fear she had said the wrong thing. But this afternoon Auntie Cris didn't seem to mind, although her face puckered into a frown, and she rocked a little harder when she answered.

'He's been dead and gone too many years for you to count, young lady.'

Helen longed to ask if he died when Johnny was a baby and what he died of but she decided that it would be best not to ask any more questions just now. It did seem odd and very sad that Auntie Cris should have lost a son and a husband both. Then the last pea dropped from Helen's fingers into the bowl and she forgot to think about anything except getting to her room to read the new *St Nicholas*.

Heedless of the white bedspread that was still fairly clean, Helen threw herself down on her stomach and opened the magazine eagerly. There was another instalment of 'The Lucky Sixpence' and two other good continued stories as well as a few short ones. Later, she'd have to read them and about 'Books and Reading' which she also liked, but now she turned over quickly to the *St Nicholas League*.

She found that in this number most of the essays that had won prizes were about 'The Book That Helped Me Most – and Why' and the Editor, in the opening paragraph, said that this subject had called out a response rarely, if ever, equalled in the history of the League.

'Even the "Dictionary" and "Spelling Book" had their advocates,' the Editor wrote, 'and one clever girl admits that her "bank book" has helped her most and tells just why.' Silly, Helen thought. She read through several of the essays and decided that she could have done much better herself writing about *The Bird's Christmas Carol*. The ones about the Bible would be bound to please the Editor, she supposed, and so would another stupid one calling *St Nicholas* a book, which it wasn't, of course. She decided that Shakespeare, *Little Women, David Copperfield* and *Pilgrim's Progress* were good ones.

She turned over the pages to see what other books the League members liked best. There was quite a list of them: *Captains Courageous, The Jungle Book*, The Little Colonel Books. She had read them all except one called *The Desert of Waiting*. The essay about this book was written by a seventeen-year-old girl who said she had, last year, moved to a strange town where she had been thrown among strangers and, at the same time, had been taken out of school by ill health. Helen felt that this girl, although she was so much older, must have felt lonely in the same way that she herself felt lonely. And the one sentence that had helped this girl most made Helen determined to read the book, too. 'From the daily tasks, that prick thee sorest, mayest thou distil some precious attar, that will gain for thee a royal entrance to the City of thy Desire.' Helen looked away from the page before her and out of the open window to the squirrel's nest in the top of the oak tree. The tiny new leaves moved restlessly, making a pattern against the sky. Yes, that was it, 'the City of thy Desire' – where everything was perfect.

Helen sighed heavily and returned to *St Nicholas*. The new competition for an essay was on the subject, 'A Seaside Adventure' or for a verse, 'A Song of the Woods'. For a moment Helen thought of changing her 'Unusual Experience' to make it happen at the seaside. She got up from the bed and took the story out of her desk drawer to read it over again. And then she remembered that she didn't want to show it to her father and that he would have to sign it as 'original'. Perhaps it would be better never to show it to anyone.

She sat down and, after several bad starts, wrote a poem, 'A Song of the Woods', in twenty-five lines. She read them through several times and, after the third time, which was always the final test, she began to feel that they really were quite good – good enough even to show to her father. Then she could send them off to New York in the morning. With this comforting thought, she returned to the bed and the stories she had skipped over.

It was beginning to get dark when Helen came to 'Books and Reading'. This month it was about the author of *The Conquest of Peru* and *The Conquest of Mexico*. He really did sound like a funny guy, Helen decided. When he was writing, he locked himself in his library with a cake of soap at which he kept nibbling, and this was because he thought people ought to be clean inside as well as out. But he was also a great man and a hero. He was mostly blind – one eye had been injured in his youth and the other eventually failed. 'It is an inspiring record,' Miss Hawthorne, who wrote the article, said, 'one that puts a glow into your heart as heroism always does.'

Helen got up from the bed in a dream. Now there were three books to get from the library, *The Desert of Waiting*, *The Conquest of Peru*, and *The Conquest of Mexico*. She might find that the history ones would be too much like school books, but it would be interesting to see what an author like William Prescott would say – a funny guy who was also a hero.

Auntie Cris's voice came from the kitchen – a faraway sound that Helen heard but hardly noticed for some time. Then the voice came nearer and increased to an angry roar. Helen rushed to the door. 'Coming, coming, *coming*,' she called. At all costs Auntie Cris must be prevented from climbing up the stairs. Helen's room had now become even more her secret place – her own City of Desire.

CHAPTER SIX

An Unusual Experience

ON the day after Helen had spent the afternoon with *St Nicholas* and had written her poem, she got up early so that she could copy it out carefully and get her father to sign it as original. Then, on her way to school, she put it into the letter-box with the feeling that a silver badge was as good as won. She had hoped her father would say something about it, perhaps even that it was a most beautiful poem. But he hadn't – not really. He had just read it, and smiled at her and said, 'I believe it's easier at your age, Nelly, to write poems than to read them.' But he hadn't said anything more, he had just written the words 'Original work' and his name, and handed the paper back to her. It was always possible that he had been especially worried at that moment about a doctor's bill or something else, and when he was worried he was very unnoticing. She had almost asked him if he liked the poem, but she was half afraid that he didn't and, besides, she wanted to get off to school promptly.

Well, she would have to wait until the September *St Nicholas* to know about her badge. The September number should arrive about August the 20th, and that would help some, but it was much too long to wait all the same. There would be all of May with school going on and on, all of June – It was true that holidays would start before the end, but that was the month when her mother was going to have her new operation and that meant that they would all stay at home in Newton Lowlands for June, July and August. Barbara Buckingham always went away to the seaside for at least a month, as most girls did. But then Barbara wasn't much fun any more. She had new friends in her own school and always wanted to play the silly little girl games that Helen felt herself to have outgrown.

It turned out that May was a dull month, just as Helen had known it would be. The days dragged by and the only good thing that happened was a leaflet that came in the mail, saying that Helen Hamilton was now a Member of the *St Nicholas League*. There was also a small badge with a pin so that she could put it on her coat. But she decided to wait until she had her poem printed before she started people asking questions about the badge. She put it carefully away in her desk drawer. Then, at last, exactly on the twentieth, the June *St Nicholas* came. After that things were a little better, but the first days of June seemed endless. Helen kept thinking about her troubles and she was still thinking about them as she walked home from school one noontime not long before the beginning of the holidays.

It was all very well to be a hero when you had something to be a hero about, something important to do to win through to the City of Desire the way the girl in the book did, but to have nothing to do that mattered, no friends, and even no mother was just emptiness and you couldn't fight against emptiness. It was just something you had to accept and not cry over. The June day was warm and Helen took off her sweater and tried skipping which was often a cheering thing to do, but today it only made her hot and tired. She couldn't help remembering how she was The Funny Guy to every single person in her grade – even, Helen sometimes thought, to Miss Perkins herself. That couldn't be true, of course, because lately Miss Perkins had been very strict with Susan and Robert. Of course it hadn't made any difference.

They had just teased her more outside of school than in it.

Just as Helen banged through the door into the kitchen, she remembered that it was Tuesday, the day on which school was always closed in the afternoon. Perhaps it would be a good idea to take the June *St Nicholas* and go down through the woods to the river, and, if she could manage it, she might hide her bathing suit under her dress. This thought made her much more cheerful. Of course she didn't have to go in swimming, but if she got very hot, she could walk along to the mill pond and have just a small quick plunge. The other children from school might be there and they might not. She would just have to face that if it happened. The kitchen smelt of fresh doughnuts and she knew that she would have two with a large piece of cheese for lunch. Helen forgot all her troubles as she sat down opposite Auntie Cris.

After lunch Helen discovered that Auntie Cris had some afternoon plans for Helen, too. There were dishes to be dried and then a few errands at the store, and it was nearly three when Helen, with her copy of *St Nicholas* under her arm, and her bathing suit held under her dress, pushed through the tangle of willow shrubs and blackberry bushes that crowded across the narrow path through the woods. It was hot and still. Helen kept stopping to listen. Birds chirped sleepily and there was always the buzzing of insects, but she could hear no sound of children's voices, even in the distance. She came at last to her favourite private place – a soft green bank near where the stream emptied itself with a pleasant gurgling noise into the mill pond. Once there had been a mill at this very spot, but now bits of the old mill wheel and the ruin of a wooden building were all that were left of it.

Helen sat down on the sunny side of the bank with her back against the grey wall and turned over the pages of *St*

Nicholas. Before long she had finished all the stories she hadn't read and she wished she had had time to get a book from the library. If only the July number had come a few days early. She turned over on her stomach to go through the magazine for a last time and that was how she happened to discover the advertisement that said 'Win a Bicycle' in bold letters. Then it went on to say that there was one boy's bicycle and one girl's bicycle to be won and that all any enterprising boy or girl had to do was to sell Christmas cards during the summer. 'The cards will come to you by mail,' it said, 'if you fill in the coupon and send it to the address given below. For every packet of twelve cards (with envelopes) which you sell and for which you will receive twenty-five cents, you have only to send us twenty cents so that, even if you don't win the bicycle, which will be awarded on September the 1st to the boy or girl who has sold the most Christmas cards in the months of June, July and August, you can still be earning money all the time.' Helen read these magic words over. Yes, all you had to do was to fill in the coupon and send it to the company who made the cards. You didn't even have to send a two-cent stamp for reply as you did in so many of the coupon advertisements. Of course a lot of June had gone already, but it would be something to do for the summer and perhaps Barbara Buckingham would help with the selling until she went away to the beach in August. Barbara had lots of relations who were rich and must need a great many Christmas cards. If Helen worked *very* hard she might win a beautiful bicycle like the one in the picture.

The very thought of this made Helen want to get started at once. She jumped up and was about to go back home through the wood path when she realized how hot and prickly she was and how nice it would be to have a swim first. The sun felt warm on her bare skin as she slipped off her clothes and buttoned on her bathing suit.

When she tried the water with her toes it was as cold as ice but, once she had stopped paddling, held her breath and plunged in, it began to feel warm and comfortable. She swam along the shore away from the mill and then thought how pleasant it would be to go all the way around the pond. It wouldn't take very long and if she didn't go out too far, the water was quite shallow and safe. She struck out slowly and swam lazily, then turned over and floated on her back to look up through the lacy green trees to the pale blue sky above them. When, at last, she reached the shore opposite the mill, she thought she heard voices and her heart stood still in sudden panic. She climbed out on the bank to listen but the only sound was the steady drumming of a woodpecker in a nearby tree. She must have imagined the voices, she thought, as she slipped happily back into the water and swam on and on in the green silence.

The evening shadows were lengthening when Helen splashed out of the water and up to the ruin of the old mill. She went around it cautiously feeling for comfortable steps for her bare feet. When she came to the spot where she had undressed, she looked around for her clothes. She was sure she had left them in a neat pile with the copy of *St Nicholas* on top for a marker. The magazine lay face downwards on the grass but there was no sign of the clothes anywhere. Helen searched and searched; but they had completely disappeared.

A breeze lifted the leaves in the trees overhead and the flickering sunlight had lost its afternoon warmth. Helen stood shivering and miserable. She must try to think what to do. She knew that if she went home in her bathing suit, she would get a never-to-be-forgotten scolding from Auntie Cris who wouldn't, for one moment, have allowed her to go swimming so early in the year. She always said the Fourth of July was plenty soon enough.

Water ran down Helen's legs in streams from her bathing suit and dripped like cold tears on to her bare toes. What could she do? Spend the night in the old mill? They said it was full of ghosts and bats. No, anything would be better than that, even the worst punishment in the world. But she hated to start out along the brambly path. She sat down with her back against the wall that still held a little of the sun's warmth, and tried to think. And now she noticed for the first time that mist was rising in little curls from the water. It crept up the bank and began to close in around her. Perhaps the clothes were hidden quite near, but she didn't dare to look for them in the misty greyness that made everything strange and unfamiliar. Most likely the clothes had been stolen by a tramp, or worse, by Robert Busby and Susan and the others, and had been taken miles away.

'Tears won't help me now,' Helen said out loud, remembering the words from some book she had read, and the ordinary sound of them in the silence seemed to give her courage. But she must do something. The mist was growing thicker every moment and the June night was cold. What would Auntie Cris do to punish her? Worse, what would her father say? It didn't matter. She would have to face it. She would have to go home in her wet bathing suit while she could still see the path through the brambles. She got to her feet and, just as she started to push her way through the undergrowth, she heard the unmistakable sound of someone running. Then a voice called, 'Helen – '

For a moment Helen did not dare to answer. It might be Robert or Susan come back to tease The Funny Guy and see the end of their sport. But when the call came again, it sounded urgent and friendly. This time Helen called out an answer and her own voice sounded very loud in the silence. A second later, a face appeared out of the

mist and it was, unmistakably, the face of Betty Higgins.

'Oh, I'm so glad I got to you in time,' she gasped. 'It's been awful. But let's not waste any time. The others will be furious if they find out what I've done and they'll be along any moment now.' She handed Helen a bundle of clothes. 'They're all here I think. Put them on quick and then we'd better go on back towards Centre Newton and swing around home the long way. Otherwise we'll run smack into them.'

She sounded breathless, and Helen didn't stop to ask questions but hurried into her clothes.

'You're shivering,' Betty said. 'It's awfully cold and foggy here by the pond.' She pulled off her sweater and Helen took it without protest. Then, together they hurried along the path that ran around the pond until it branched

off at the other end to join the main road at Centre Newton.

It was after six when the two girls came in sight of Helen's house, and stopped for a moment to catch their breath.

'I don't know how to thank you,' Helen said shyly.

'You'd thank me more if I'd been quicker, or tried to stop them in the beginning. But I just didn't think. Susan kind of leads you on – and on – until you don't know what you are doing, and Robert's the same. The rest of us just tag along. It seemed wonderful fun when it all started, but by the time it began to get misty and late I thought of you there all alone and I had to try to find you.'

'I – I was scared stiff,' Helen admitted.

'Anybody would have been – even Lancelot or Galahad,' Betty said quickly. 'Well, I've got to dash.'

Helen giggled at the thought of Lancelot and Galahad caught out in their bathing suits. Then suddenly she was serious again. 'Won't the others murder you for this?' she asked.

'I don't think they'll know who did it. They hid the clothes in the woods. I said I had to go home early and left as soon as I could. I did go home, too – but just to get my sweater. I hope I wasn't too late – I mean I hope you don't catch cold or anything.'

'Oh, no. I'm warm now. Here's your sweater.'

'No, keep it for now. I'll go home from school with you tomorrow and pick it up.'

Helen walked the rest of the way up Hyde Street in a dream of happiness. She had always liked Betty Higgins, but since she was Susan's best friend it seemed natural that she had to be Helen's enemy, too. And now she was Helen's friend. There was no mistake about that. She had even said she would walk home from school with Helen tomorrow. That was almost the best part of it all – even better than the rescue because no one would ever know about that.

Helen did not get either a cold or a scolding. Auntie Cris was busy in the kitchen when Helen crept in through the cellar door and hung her tell-tale suit to dry by the furnace. It had been lit by Danny, the handyman, as it always was when the nights were cold, in order to take the chill out of the house for Auntie's rheumatism. By the greatest good luck, supper was late because Helen's father had telephoned to say that he could not get home until seven. And that was why Auntie Cris, in a flutter of preparations in the kitchen, was too busy even to notice that Helen's hair showed the effects of an afternoon bath. Then, with supper so late, Helen could have a few minutes of vigorous rubbing in front of the open door of the furnace, and make the pigtails look exactly as they always did. Helen knew that she owed this wonderful escape to her new friend and, that night, before she climbed into bed, she promised God, in her prayers, that she would never forget Betty Higgins or cease to be grateful, no matter what happened – never so long as they both lived.

Early the next morning Helen went out and mailed the Christmas card coupon in a letter to the Associated Greeting Card Company in New York. She felt very happy. She had had a miraculous escape from grave danger. She was about to earn a new bicycle. And, best of all, she was going to have Betty Higgins to walk home with her after school.

But Betty wasn't in school and when, after a great deal of serious thought, Helen went around to Betty's house in Birch Road with the sweater, she learned from Mrs Higgins, who came to the door herself, that Betty was in bed with a cold and a temperature and that it would probably be a few days before she could go back to school.

Mrs Higgins who, Helen thought, looked anxious, shut the door so quickly that Helen didn't have time to think of any of the questions that came crowding into her mind a minute later. She longed to ring the bell and ask if she could go in to see Betty after school the next day or even just stop by and ask how she was. But Helen knew that she mustn't call Mrs Higgins to the door again and by the time she had walked home, she had begun to believe that Betty didn't want to see her – that she only wanted to see Susan and the others; not The Funny Guy. The sweater had been an excuse to call, but now there was no reason, no reason at all, why Helen should go to Betty's house again. The sweater – Suddenly the awful realization came to Helen – *that* was why Mrs Higgins had shut the door so quickly. *That* was the reason why Betty had caught a cold. She had needed the sweater herself and Helen should never have taken it away from her. Helen felt hot with shame. Would Betty get pneumonia? Would she even die?

For the next two days Helen found it very difficult to do anything at all. She couldn't keep her mind on her lessons at school and she couldn't pay attention to anything she did at home. Auntie Cris got cross and gave her syrup of figs because she wasn't hungry. At school no one spoke of the adventure by the mill pond and, for a time, no one even remembered to call her The Funny Guy. Betty did not come back to school and Helen had to learn how she was from the snatches of talk of the other children. First Betty was said to be better and then she was worse. Helen was so worried that even the arrival of the large bundle of Christmas cards with a letter of instructions from the Associated Greeting Card Co. didn't seem very exciting and, for a long time, the parcel lay untouched on her desk.

Every day holidays came nearer, and still Betty didn't

come back to school. Then, on Friday morning of the next to the last week of school, Helen met Barbara Buckingham whose school had already ended. Helen hadn't even thought of Barbara since the day of the great adventure, and she felt a little guilty when Barbara asked her if she had been ill. Helen couldn't think what to say until she remembered the Christmas cards and then she began to talk about them in a sudden rush of words. After asking a great many questions, Barbara agreed to go out with Helen the very next day which would be a Saturday and see how many they could sell. Since Barbara already had a bicycle, she agreed to take a share of the money they would earn, and leave the prize for Helen.

That afternoon at school, Helen heard Susan tell another girl that, though Betty was much better, her mother had decided to take her away to the seaside where they had a summer cottage. There was no hope now that she would come back to school before the new term started in September.

That night after Helen had gone to bed, she lay watching the pattern of light on her ceiling. The leaves on the oak tree were now large enough to make dark shadows and the light that came in from the street lamp at the corner of Hyde Street beyond the garden seemed pale and shimmering. Why was it that the bright happy things were always blotted out with worrying things just the way the tree leaves had come to blot out the light on the slanting ceiling? Helen wanted to turn her face into the pillow and have what Auntie Cris called 'a good cry and feel better', when she heard someone coming slowly up the stairs to her room. At first she thought it was Auntie Cris and then, in a rush of happiness, she knew that it was her father.

'Are you awake, Nelly?' he asked as he came in and sat down on the edge of her bed.

'Oh, yes,' Helen said quickly as she moved over and reached out for his hand.

For a long time they didn't speak again but the silence was comfortable and Helen began to feel sleepy. Then her father said quietly, 'Tomorrow your mother is going to have her operation. The doctor is very sure it will make her well, but I want you to pray for her, Nelly dear.'

Helen held the large hand tight in both of hers for a moment. Then her father stooped to kiss her and left as unexpectedly as he had come.

Helen was very sleepy now but she climbed out of bed to make her new special prayer.

CHAPTER SEVEN

Failure and Success

WHEN Helen came down to breakfast on Saturday morning, her father had already left, and Auntie Cris was in a silent mood. Helen, for once, didn't have anything to say either. She couldn't tell Auntie about the Christmas card expedition because she had a feeling that Auntie wouldn't approve. She never did approve of doing anything different and was apt to say, 'Have you got your father's permission?' – so it was just as well not to mention such things. For some reason Helen didn't want to speak about her mother's operation either. Auntie Cris looked so gloomy that she might say some awful thing that Helen didn't want to hear. She hurried through her bacon and eggs and even drank up all her milk without being told to. Afterwards, she finished her Saturday morning work in record time.

Far away in the distance, Helen could hear the clock in the tower of the Congregational Church striking ten as she walked up the path to Barbara Buckingham's front door. For a moment she stood on the porch, shut her eyes and crossed her fingers tight, in order to make the wish that Barbara would come to the door herself. Then she pushed the bell. Almost at once it flew open and a maid in a pink uniform with a clean white apron and stiff starched cap frowned down at her. Every time the door of the Buckingham house flew open to reveal Maria, pink or blue in the morning, or black in the afternoon, Helen had to fight back an impulse to turn and run away. Maria had always been disapproving when Helen had lived with Barbara, and, this Saturday morning, Maria was more disapproving than ever.

'What are you doing here at this hour?' she asked. 'Goodness gracious, Barbara isn't out of bed yet. I take it you do want to see Barbara though you don't seem to have any tongue this morning.'

Helen ignored the question. Of course she wanted to see Barbara. 'Not up yet,' she repeated stupidly. She was quite unable to believe that Barbara, or anyone, could still be in bed unless there was something wrong with them.

'You heard me,' Maria said rudely. She started to close the door. 'I'm very busy. Now you run along and come back in an hour or two. Barbara's just going to have her breakfast now.'

'Can't I just see her for a minute?' Helen asked desperately. But the door had already closed before she had finished speaking.

This disaster completely upset all Helen's plans. How could they ever get any calls made, and Christmas cards sold, before lunch? And in the afternoon people were much more likely to be out. She walked home slowly and discussed the problem with Cindy who was waiting for her on the gate post. He seemed to agree that she ought to start out by herself and not wait for Barbara. It would be twice as hard. But if she must, she must. She shut her eyes and kept her hand on Cindy's soft back as she repeated slowly, 'From the daily tasks that prick thee sorest, mayest thou distil some precious attar, that will gain for thee a royal entrance to the City of thy Desire.'

Then she turned quickly and went into the house. She crept up the stairs quietly so that Auntie wouldn't hear her and think of something else to be done. Safely in her room, she put several packets of cards into an old shopping bag, brushed her hair, and then crept down again, let herself out of the house without slamming the screen door, and hurried down the path. She had already decided that the best plan would be to start far away at the other end of town and then, by the time she came to people she knew, she would be used to it and it wouldn't be quite so hard.

The sun shone brightly and there was a fresh morning smell in the air. Helen sniffed happily. Perhaps the Christmas cards could be an excuse to stop at Betty's house and ask how she was. It was a little longer to go that way, but Helen wasn't in a great hurry now. She walked along Birch Road and turned in the path at number sixteen quickly while she still felt brave enough. Even so, she gripped the bag tightly in her hand and tried to think just what she would say if Mrs Higgins came to the door. 'I was just out selling some Christmas cards, and I thought I would stop and ask how Betty is.' Or would it be better to say, 'Would you like to buy some Christmas cards?' – and then just casually ask about Betty afterwards.

Suddenly a voice said, 'Whatever are you muttering about? And where have you been all this time?'

Helen looked up. There at the end of the porch, in the part screened by a trumpet vine, was Betty herself. She was lying in a hammock and pushing it backwards and forwards with one hand that just reached down to the floor.

'Oh, it's you,' Helen said. And then she couldn't think of anything else to say.

Betty laughed. 'You look scared to death. Did you think I was a ghost?' she asked. 'Well, I'm not. Do come over here and sit down. I've been hoping and hoping you'd come to see me. But when you just left the sweater, I was afraid you thought I was contagious or something.'

'Oh, no. But everyone said you were awfully sick and I

didn't want to be a nuisance – I mean, I was afraid your mother would mind – '

'Well, anyway, you're here now,' Betty said sensibly. 'Can't you stay and play a game of Parcheesi with me? I'm supposed to stay in this hateful hammock and I get so *bored*. I think I've read every book in the Public Library.'

Helen walked across the porch on tiptoe. She felt a little shy so she looked down at the pile of books on the floor, and a second even higher stack on the wicker table. Then she forgot to answer the question Betty had asked her because she couldn't think of anything except the books.

'Oh, do tell me what ones you like best. I seem never to get enough good ones and Miss Singleton in the library is always telling me that I won't like the ones that I know I will – '

'I like family stories mostly – The Little Colonel books and all the Alcott ones, but lately I've been reading adventure and nature books. *Wild Life in the Rockies* is a good one and *The Lure of the Labrador Wild*. You see, we were all going to camp in the Rockies this summer and now we aren't. We're just going back to Quonset instead.'

Betty stopped suddenly and turned her head away. Helen wanted to ask her what was the matter. It seemed to Helen that a summer at the beach was about as perfect as anyone could have. She wanted to ask Betty a hundred questions. But they might be the wrong ones and they might make her really cry. Instead she said quickly, 'Let's play a game of Parcheesi.'

She waited anxiously and after a minute Betty turned back again and said, 'Yes, let's.'

Helen got out the board and put it on the table after she had moved it near the hammock. They had been playing their game for some time before Helen remembered the

Christmas cards. Oh, well, it didn't matter. She couldn't stop now. After lunch would probably do just as well and then she might have Barbara for company.

At half past eleven, Mrs Higgins came out with an eggnog for Betty, a large glass of lemonade for Helen, and a plate of cookies for both of them.

'You're Helen Hamilton, aren't you?' she asked pleasantly.

'Yes,' Helen answered, and then tried to think of something else to say. All morning, even with the fun of the game, Helen had been having a guilty feeling whenever she looked at Betty's pale face and thin hands. If Helen hadn't borrowed the sweater, then probably Betty wouldn't have got a cold and all this illness would never have happened. Did Mrs Higgins think this, too? Helen made herself look up, but Mrs Higgins was smiling and there was nothing but interest and friendliness in her face.

'How is your mother?' she now asked.

Usually Helen hated this question but, in some way that she couldn't explain, she was very pleased that Betty's mother had asked it. Besides, today, she had something definite and hopeful to say. 'She's having an operation. She's had quite a lot already, you know, but this is a new doctor and he thinks – maybe – maybe he can get her really well.'

Helen felt the old familiar lump in her throat and her cheeks flushed pink. But Mrs Higgins didn't seem to notice. She said quickly, 'Now that really is good news. Well, I must get on with my work.' She turned to go into the house and then stopped to look back and say, 'It's so boring for Betty having to rest all the time. I hope you'll come in often to see her – We're going to get her away to the seaside as soon as she can travel but that probably won't be for a week or two.'

'I think you're lucky to be going to Quonset,' Helen said when they were alone again.

'Yes,' Betty said, 'only I've been there every summer since I can remember and this year Daddy had this idea about seeing the Rockies. Only – only I'm not strong enough, the doctor says.'

Helen couldn't think of anything to say except that she thought Quonset a million times better than Newton Lowlands. And then she found herself telling Betty how she had to stay at home and about the Christmas cards, too. Betty was interested in that, and said she wished she had *St Nicholas*. And, after they had finished their eggnog and lemonade and eaten all the cookies, they didn't play Parcheesi any more because there seemed to be so much to talk about.

It was almost one o'clock when Helen left and, as she walked home in the midday heat, she felt happier than she had for a long time. She liked everything about Betty. Helen had carried the tray in to Mrs Higgins who was cooking in the kitchen and she had decided that it was a very nice house, full of comfortable and homelike things. Helen also liked Betty's mother who seemed much more like her own mother than Auntie Cris or Mrs Buckingham. But, above all, she liked Betty herself. Betty looked pretty, even now that she was so thin and pale. Her hair was dark and curly and her eyes blue and bright. What was more she liked to do the same things and to read the same books.

Helen swung the old shopping bag absent-mindedly and never once thought about the Christmas cards inside it until she got home and Auntie said, 'Barbara Buckingham's been by looking for you. I told her I didn't know where in tunket you'd gone to. At that she flounced out of here as if I'd spanked her. That girl's a great one for putting on airs, I always did think.'

'She didn't say whether or not she'd be back this afternoon, did she?'

'Not she. No indeedy.'

On any other day, this news would have worried Helen
very much but today everything was different. She decided that she would even dare to face Maria in her black
uniform, if Barbara didn't come back.

But just as Helen was drying the last dish and listening
to Auntie Cris singing, *Washed in the Blood of the Lamb*,
Barbara knocked at the back door. Then there were a few
anxious moments when Auntie Cris wanted to know
where they were off to and Helen muttered something
about having some errands to do which was true in a way.
Fortunately, as Auntie Cris wasn't really interested or
even listening, Helen and Barbara were able to escape
without any more questions.

It had been agreed that Helen would do all the talking
and actual selling since neither of them felt sure that Mrs
Buckingham would approve of this venture any more
than Auntie Cris. Mrs Buckingham often disapproved of
things and Helen thought it just as well not to have Barbara take an active part. When they had made the plans,
Helen had felt rather pleased and important to be the
leader of the expedition but when, at last, they reached
the other side of town and started up the walk to the first
house on Walnut Street, Helen wished with all her heart
that she had not taken quite the whole burden of re-
sponsibility.

The woman who opened the door shut it again almost
tight and peered at them through the crack. Helen said
quickly, 'We have some very nice Christmas cards – '

'Selling, are you?' the woman said crossly and slammed
the door before they could say another word.

Anyway, the first call was over. Barbara wanted to give
up the idea altogether. 'No one wants to *buy* things,' she

said. 'My mother never buys things at the door, either.'

But Helen felt certain that some people would want to see the Christmas cards. Even Auntie Cris often looked at things. And if anyone looked, they couldn't help buying because the cards were so beautiful and there were twelve large cards with envelopes for twenty-five cents which wasn't at all expensive.

But at the next house, the woman who opened the door shut it even more quickly. 'Can't you read?' she asked crossly. 'There's a notice plain as a pike-staff on the gate.'

Helen and Barbara hurried back down the path and looked at the gate. A white enamel sign said, in large blue letters, 'No Peddlers Allowed'.

'I didn't see that at all, did you?' Barbara asked in a hushed voice.

'No. But even if I had, I would never have thought of us as *peddlers*,' Helen said. This was much worse than she had expected, but if she said so, Barbara would give up and go home and she felt that she couldn't possibly go on all alone. 'I don't think they'll all be like those,' she went on quickly, trying very hard to sound cheerful. 'Let's make ten calls and then we'll see how people really feel.'

'*Ten*,' Barbara grumbled. 'That's a terrible lot.'

'We've got to give ourselves a test,' Helen said stoutly.

'Oh, all right. Let's hurry up then. I'd rather go home and play.'

They went from door to door, but it was obvious, after their first ten calls, that, whether there was a sign or not, most of the housewives and all of the maids didn't have the least interest in Christmas cards on a warm day in June.

Helen and Barbara were very tired and hot when the ten

calls had been made. They decided to walk the few blocks to the drug store and buy two ice-cream cones. This was possible because they had sold two packets to one old lady who had called them, 'My little dears'. This made a total sale of fifty cents and, out of that, they could keep ten cents for themselves – that made two ice-cream cones. But Helen couldn't help thinking, as she lapped the beautiful pink mound of ice-cream slowly, that it would be too bad if all their profits were eaten up as soon as they earned them.

When they had finished, and climbed down from their stools by the drug store counter, Barbara said she had decided to go home. Helen had expected this, and she had been thinking very hard.

'If I buy us another cone, will you go back with me?'

'How can you?'

'I'll *borrow* five cents and then pay it back when we sell one more.'

'Oh, all right then,' Barbara agreed grudgingly. This time they took turns lapping the ice-cream and biting the cone.

'I've got a plan,' Helen said, at last, when they climbed down from their seats a second time. She knew she would have to keep Barbara interested. There were still twenty-three unsold packets out of the original twenty-five and she had hoped to sell hundreds and hundreds and win the bicycle for selling more than anyone else.

'What is it?' Barbara felt a little better after her ice-cream and she turned to Helen expectantly.

'Well, I've been thinking that Mother always used to buy flowers and things if anyone came selling them *for* something.'

'What do you mean *"for something"*?'

'Well, I was thinking we could say that we were selling the Christmas cards for the benefit of the Boston Baby

Hospital. I'm sure people would be more interested then.'

'Yes, but we wouldn't be. If you think I'm going to give up my half of the money just so you can save up for your bicycle – '

Her voice had risen dangerously and Helen said quickly, 'No, of course not. We could give a penny, maybe, out of each five cents and,' she looked at Barbara's frowning face, and went on quickly, 'the penny would come out of my share since I'm maybe going to win the bicycle.'

'But that isn't very much for the Baby Hospital, is it?'

'It's enough to be able to *say* it,' Helen said firmly. They were approaching the first house on Elm Street and Helen wasn't quite so sure about her plan as she had been when she first thought of it in the drug store.

But they soon discovered that the words 'Boston Baby Hospital' were as magic as *abracadabra*. Some people still shut the door in their faces but more and more of them opened it wide, some even asked them to come inside and wait while they went to get their purses.

And there was one lady who gave them lemonade and cookies. Barbara and Helen sat on the railing of the porch to drink it while the lady, who said her name was Mrs Cadwalader Brown, looked down at them. She was very tall and had a deep voice.

'I'm glad my maid was out this afternoon. She always sends peddlers away. But I do think you deserve to make many sales. If more children took an interest in the work of the Baby Hospital, we wouldn't have so many sick babies.'

Helen began to be a little worried. She drank up her lemonade quickly and kicked Barbara to make her hurry up, too. But Barbara didn't pay any attention. She looked up at Mrs Cadwalader Brown and said in her best grown-up voice, 'Yes, that's what my mother says.'

'How nice,' Mrs Brown boomed. 'Now what is your name?'

Helen gave another hard kick which Barbara couldn't ignore. She kicked back even harder and answered at once, 'Barbara Buckingham, and my friend is Helen Hamilton.'

'Oh, yes. I think Mrs Buckingham is on my Church Committee. How very nice. Well, girls, I expect you want to carry on with your good work.' She took the glasses and, after smiling down at them once more, turned and went inside.

When they got out of sight of Mrs Brown's house, Barbara said, 'Why did you keep on kicking me? You are a horrid person and I'm going to tell my mother.'

'I wanted you *not* to tell our names. Suppose she tells your mother. How will you like that, Miss Smarty?'

'Well, I couldn't *not* answer when she asked me, could I?'

'You always talk too much,' Helen answered crossly and for all of five minutes they didn't speak another word to each other. But as the sales continued, they both felt better and better. At half past five when they walked home, very dusty, hot and tired, they had sold all their cards and a large amount of money jingled in the bottom of Helen's shopping bag.

Helen had forgotten her anxiety about Mrs Cadwalader Brown. '*Now*, what do you think of my plan?' she asked as they stopped to count out the money under the oak tree that stood in the middle of the path through the field that was the short cut home.

'It was wonderful,' Barbara said without a moment's hesitation. 'You'll write for some more cards, won't you? And let's get as many sold as we can before I go away.'

Helen went home very happy and she was almost too

sleepy to write her letter to the Associated Greeting Card Co. and make up her accounts after supper.

Perhaps it was a good thing to be tired, Helen thought, as she climbed into bed. If you were so sleepy that your eyes wouldn't stay open then you couldn't even think about Father who hadn't come home from the hospital, and Mother who had had her operation.

Auntie Cris had said there wasn't any news.

CHAPTER EIGHT

Prayers and a Poem

'WAKE up, Helen. Wake up, child!'

But Helen was riding down a never-ending hill on a beautiful new bicycle. The wind rushed past her face, and she could feel the bicycle shake beneath her like an excited steed.

Then suddenly she felt something tugging at her shoulder, like a giant hand trying to hold her back. She pedalled furiously trying to get away from the awful thing that had come down out of the clear blue sky to spoil everything.

'Helen. *Helen*. My goodness gracious me. Will you never wake up?'

Now Helen heard at last. The bicycle faded back into the dream and she sat up. Her room had a faint pink glow.

'What's the matter?' she said, clutching out in sudden fear. 'Is the house on fire?' Auntie Cris, in her green dressing-gown and with her hair in a funny little braid behind, looked faintly pink. Helen rubbed her eyes.

'No, dear. That's the sunrise. It's glorious, a sign from the Almighty I wouldn't wonder. But get up and put on your bathrobe and slippers. Your father's on the telephone and wants to speak to you.'

'Daddy. But *what, where*, I mean – '

'Never mind now, child.' Auntie Cris was being her very nicest. Her voice had a hushed sound as it did in church, when she helped Helen find the place in the hymnal. Helen jumped out of bed, shuffled her feet into her bedroom slippers, and reached for her bathrobe in one quick move.

'You run along ahead, Helen. My old legs are too slow.'

Helen didn't need a second invitation. She flew down the two flights of stairs into the hall and then on into the little room beyond it that she loved. Even as she reached for the telephone she was conscious of the smell of her father's pipes on the table near the desk. It seemed right to be talking to him from his own den. She could even see their favourite book of poems in the bookcase. It had a green cover and fancy lettering in gold but she never could remember its name.

She sat down in the large worn leather chair and said, 'Hello,' in a very loud voice.

'Is that you, Nelly?' Her father's voice sounded far away and tired.

'Oh, yes. It's me. Where are you?'

'I'm sorry to get you and Auntie Cris out of bed so early in the morning. I couldn't call you last night because I stayed at the hospital. I'm just going to get some sleep now but I thought I should talk to you first. I knew you would be worried.'

Helen remembered how sleepy she had been last night and how she hadn't even had time to worry at all. She said quickly in order to hide the guilty feeling, 'I like getting up early. It's all pink from the sunrise.'

'Good. And I've good news for you. Your mother has come through the night. We think now she really will get better – '

'Oh – ' Helen suddenly wanted to cry. Why did she always want to cry at times like this when she should only be happy?

'But, Nelly, your mother was very ill when she had this operation and she is now.' He hesitated, and then went on

93

slowly. 'She is now completely exhausted. I want you to pray for her, Nelly, and I want you to be patient and good.'

He stopped suddenly and, after a moment, Helen said quickly, 'Oh, yes. You know I will, Daddy.'

'Good girl. Well now, I've got a room in a hotel near the hospital. I may get home tonight but late, after you're in bed, and only for an hour or so. I want to pick up some things I need. But I won't be home to stay for a week or more.'

'Can I, please, come and see Mother, too?' Helen asked.

'Not yet. I said you must be patient and good – '

'Yes. I know. I will be.' Helen gulped back the tears of disappointment and managed to answer her father's good-bye before the flood came.

On the landing she met Auntie Cris who was standing at the window looking out.

'I never saw the like of it,' she said.

Helen stood beside her for a moment and looked out at the flaming sky and the soft pile of clouds with neat gold edges that rose up and up over the tops of the trees. And then suddenly she wanted to be all alone to see the sunrise behind her own oak tree.

Auntie Cris turned around to say, 'It's worth getting up early to see this sight and get your father's good news, isn't it, child?' But Helen had already gone. 'Poor little tyke,' Auntie Cris said, half to herself, and then decided that, since she was up, she might as well get dressed and make herself a cup of coffee.

Safe in her own room, Helen closed the door softly and went to kneel by the window. The pink colour had gone from the sky now and it was all golden and dazzling. The oak tree looked as though it had been touched by Midas except that it wasn't stiff and hard like ordinary gold. As

94

the breeze moved the leaves gently they seemed to be dripping with light.

Helen felt the cold hard floor under her bare knees but she couldn't make herself get up and go back to bed. She wanted to make a prayer or a poem but she couldn't even think. For a long time she knelt by the window watching the golden glow fade from the sky and listening to the early morning chattering of the birds.

'Auntie,' Helen said at breakfast, 'please may I go to church with you instead of to Sunday School?'

'I thought you wanted to get your geranium for perfect attendance.'

'Well, I did get one last year and I do like church better.'

'Now whatever put that idea into your head, I'd like to know?' Auntie Cris got up and began to stack the dishes in the sink.

This was much better. It was easier to explain when Auntie Cris's bright eyes weren't looking at her over the half-glasses.

'You see,' Helen said slowly, 'I want to make a prayer to thank God for getting Mother over the operation and to ask him to make her all well as soon as possible. Somehow it's easier to pray in church with the organ and all.'

'But you don't pray when the organ's playing,' Auntie Cris answered practically.

Helen didn't want to tell the real reason. In Sunday School it was the same as ordinary school. During the prayers everyone giggled and if Susan Johnson was there she might even whisper something about The Funny Guy. 'Sunday School isn't solemn enough,' Helen said at last.

Auntie Cris turned around and looked at Helen. 'You are a funny one, and no mistake.'

Helen didn't like it when Auntie Cris called her

'funny'. She stared at a little spot of milk on the checked tablecloth and didn't look up. Then, suddenly, she had an idea. 'Besides, I do love to hear you sing, Auntie, and I can't hear you in Sunday School.'

Helen looked up now and saw that Auntie Cris was smiling. She turned back to her dishes quickly. 'Very well, then, if you think your father wouldn't mind, I've no objections. But none of your fidgets now, young lady.'

In a few moments Auntie cleared her throat and began to sing, *Love Divine, All Loves Excelling*, but after a moment she stopped suddenly to say, 'Now that I've got that stain out of your new dress, you can wear that if you want to.'

Auntie Cris stayed in her good mood all that Sunday. Towards the end of the long sermon Helen hadn't been able to keep from fidgeting a little and Auntie Cris hadn't scolded a bit. Instead she had reached for the hymnal and had let Helen turn the pages as much as she liked. Then there was chicken for lunch and in the afternoon while Auntie was having what she called 'forty winks' Helen had been able to copy out her letter to the Associated Greeting Card Co. and to count over again the pile of money in the bottom of the shopping bag. Since every packet of cards had been sold, that meant twenty-five of them at twenty-five cents each. That made six dollars and twenty-five cents. Helen read over her letter of instructions. Yes, all she had to send was 'cheque or postal order – not money – for five dollars'. That left one dollar and twenty-five cents because the person who sold the cards could keep five cents for each packet, and twenty-five times five cents made a dollar and twenty-five cents. Yes, it came right whichever way you figured it!

Helen counted out five dollars and put it in an old purse that her mother had given her long ago for dress-ups. Then she made her plans. She would get off early in the morning so that she could stop at the Post Office on the way to school and buy a postal order and a stamp for the letter. She put an extra ten cents into the old purse to pay for that. Then she counted the change. There was just a dollar. That was right because fifteen cents had been spent for three ice-cream cones and ten cents had been put into the old purse for cost of postage.

Helen found a clean white paper in her desk drawer and began to do some more figuring. She had agreed to give Barbara half of the profits for every one sold – that would be two and a half cents each, and two and a half times twenty-five was sixty-two and a half cents. But it was only fair that Barbara should pay for her ice-cream and half the cost of postage. That would make half of what was left, and half of a dollar was fifty cents. That seemed quite a lot of money and Helen felt very pleased as she put it away in the secret drawer inside her desk. Then she thought it would be a good idea to go over and give Barbara her share and show her the letter.

Barbara was sitting under a tree in her back yard reading *The Wizard of Oz*. Helen felt that she herself had outgrown the Oz books a long time ago and thought Barbara very silly to go on reading them over and over again. But today she didn't say anything. Instead, she crept up behind and showered the money into Barbara's lap.

Barbara looked cross at first and then, when she saw the money, she changed to looking pleased. Helen explained about the expenses and Barbara didn't seem to mind paying her half: 'Let's go down to the drug store right now and buy an ice-cream soda,' she said.

'I haven't got my money here,' Helen answered quickly. She didn't like to say that she didn't want to spend it. She wanted to save it and then add more and more until the whole drawer was full and she could buy something wonderful with it.

Barbara collected the money in her hand and stood up. 'Well you can go and get it while I go in and get my purse.'

'All right,' Helen agreed. She didn't want to spend her money, it was true, but it was a hot afternoon and an ice-cream soda would taste very good.

It tasted so good that, after their first one, Helen and Barbara each had another. They cost ten cents and that made twenty cents each. Then, as they started to leave the drug store Barbara stopped at the sweet counter, 'I've only got thirty cents left,' she said grandly. 'I might as well get some candy to take home.'

Helen decided that she was going to save her thirty cents. She watched Barbara spend her money as though it didn't matter at all. Then, as Barbara was stuffing the sweets into her pockets, a very familiar voice behind them said, 'Isn't The Funny Guy going to buy any? I bet *she* hasn't got any money.'

'I have too.' Helen turned around to face Robert Busby who was grinning down at her from the stool by the soda fountain. She hated to have Barbara know the horrid name he called her and she was afraid he would say it again. She pulled out her purse and showed him the money.

'All right then, buy us some sweets,' he said in a lordly voice.

Helen now saw that Susan Johnson was sitting on the stool on the other side of Robert, and she knew that he was always worse when Susan was with him. She mustn't give them a chance to tease her. She hesitated only a moment, and then handed all her money to the man who was still standing behind the counter. 'I'll take six of these, and five of these, and let's see, three of those,' she said, helping herself, without waiting to be asked.

'Here, now, what are you up to, young lady,' the man

said. Helen held out what she had chosen and he counted it up. 'One more peppermint stick,' he said, 'and we're just even.'

Robert and Susan were silenced by this magnificent display of wealth. Helen handed them each a chocolate bar and fairly flew out of the door. But Robert and Susan were too surprised to call after her.

At first, as Helen and Barbara walked home along the path by the short cut, Helen's only feeling was one of relief that Barbara hadn't noticed about The Funny Guy. But by the time they reached the oak tree, she had begun to think about the money.

And then Barbara said, 'What about the twenty-five cents for the Boston Baby Hospital?'

Helen stood still. Until that very moment she hadn't given the hospital one single thought. 'Oh, Barbara,' she said, 'why didn't you remind me? I just never thought. I forgot.'

'Well, I thought you were saving that last thirty cents after we had the sodas. But then you spent it in such a whirlwind I didn't have time to say anything, did I?'

'No.' Helen was very glad Barbara hadn't said anything just then. It would have been the worst possible moment. All the same the worst possible thing had happened, and there just wasn't any money left for the Baby Hospital.

'Well,' Barbara said, tossing back a long curl over her shoulder, 'I think it would look funny to send in twenty-five cents to the Hospital Fund. You'd better wait until you have a dollar and then it looks like something.'

'Yes, but that would mean four lots of cards and we might never get that many sold. It's a hundred packs.'

'I thought you were going to sell thousands. You'll never get your bicycle if you don't.'

Helen began to kick a stone along the dusty path. All

that day until now had been happy. But from the very moment of giving Barbara her money, everything had gone wrong, and the worst of it was that it wasn't Barbara's fault, or even Robert's, or Susan's. It was her very own. She never should have taken her money out of the drawer at all. If it was still safely there, everything would be all right. It was like what the Minister had said that morning in church about one little bad weed growing and growing and choking all the flowers in the garden.

'Perhaps you're right,' she said, at last. 'Anyway, I was going to show you the letter I'd written asking for some more cards to sell. I'm going to send it with a postal order tomorrow morning.'

'Well, your school ends on Tuesday, doesn't it? The cards'll probably come by Wednesday and then we can start right in again. If we sell the next lot in one day like we did the last lot, then you'll have your Baby Hospital money and our money in no time.'

Yes, Helen couldn't help thinking, you'll have *your* money, but all mine, or nearly all of it, will have to go to the Baby Hospital and maybe I'll never win the bicycle at all.

As Helen undressed that night she looked out at the black sky and the far-away bright stars above the oak tree. How different it all was from the blaze of fiery sunrise. Suddenly she wanted her mother. But it was no good wanting: praying and hoping and waiting were all that mattered, as her father had told her. If only he had come home early, she could have talked to him about the Christmas cards. He would understand and tell her what to do. But he wouldn't want her to be awake if he came in late and he wouldn't be back again for a whole week.

She put on her nightgown and stood at the window listening to the small night sounds. What was it her father had said about poems, 'It's easier, at your age, to write them, than to read them, isn't it?' Yes, that was true because every poet made a kind of music of his own that you couldn't understand – unless you had someone like a father to help you.

Well, her father wasn't there to read her a poem or to hear about all the worrying things that had happened. Suddenly, she remembered the little green book with fancy gold lettering that was on the bookshelf in the den. Without stopping to think, she stepped into her slippers and crept down the stairs. It was easy to find the book, even in the darkness, because she had got it for her father so many times. And it would be as well not to put on the light for fear Auntie Cris would see it and come and ask her whatever she was up to.

Safe upstairs, she crept into bed leaving the gas light on. It was just over her head and she could reach up and turn it off when she finished.

She found the poem easily because her father had left the blue ribbon marker in that very page. It was called *Night* and it was written by William Blake.

> The sun descending in the west,
>   The evening star does shine;
> The birds are silent in their nest,
>   And I must seek for mine.
> The moon, like a flower,
>   In heaven's high tower,
> With silent delight
>   Sits and smiles on the night.

Helen read the verse over slowly. It was simple and comforting and easy to understand. She tried to read the other verses but they were harder and she couldn't remember what her father had said about them, so she went back to the first and read it again and again until she knew it by heart. Then she reached up and turned off the light. She hadn't said her prayers but then she had said a great many in church. Tonight her prayer would be a poem. She said it over slowly once more, and then she forgot all the worrying things and fell asleep.

CHAPTER NINE

The Funny Guy Again

THERE is something special about the last two days of school, Helen thought, as she ate her breakfast on Monday morning, and there is something even more special about the beginning of a summer holiday even if it isn't going to be a very exciting one. All her worries that were so serious last night seemed much less serious this morning. She had the letter ready to mail to the Associated Greeting Card Co. and, luckily, she had put the ten cents to pay for the postal order and the stamp into the old purse with the five dollars. She kept looking at the alarm clock on the mantelpiece over the stove. But it was all right; she was early, and she would have plenty of time to stop at the Post Office on her way to school.

As she skipped along Hyde Street she saw Mr Walsh coming around the corner. He waved and beckoned but she knew she mustn't stop to talk so she waved back but didn't cross the road. When he came nearer he called out, 'Your *St Nicholas Magazine*'s come.'

At that Helen dashed across to him, took the familiar brown parcel and hurried on her way. 'I'm sorry,' she called back to him, 'I've got an important errand to do before school and I don't want to be late.'

Mr Walsh smiled. 'That's all right, young lady, I'd rather stop for a gossip when my bag's empty in the afternoon than chock-a-block the way it is this morning.'

Helen was in very good time. She got the letter safely mailed and, when she passed the fence by the church, there wasn't a single head to be seen. Inside the building she found Miss Perkins working at her desk but no one else in the schoolroom. Miss Perkins looked up.

'Oh, it's you, Helen. Good morning. How nice and early you are. Will you write out these instructions for me on the blackboard, please? Make your writing round and clear so everyone can read them.'

Helen took the paper Miss Perkins handed her. Usually she liked to do special jobs for Miss Perkins but today she wanted to look at *St Nicholas*. Now she wouldn't have time to read any of it until break. She would never dare to open it in class again.

The list of instructions were the same as they always were on the next to the last day of school – all about clearing out desks, emptying ink wells, stacking up books, and washing out paint boxes. Still it was good to think that even on Monday, lessons were almost over and that there wouldn't be any more for two and a half whole months.

The excitement of doing last things made the morning fly by until break and then, at last, Helen could slip away from the others, who were playing tag, and climb up on the fence to read her *St Nicholas*. The same advertisement to earn easy money and maybe win a bicycle was still there and Helen was relieved to find it. Something might have happened to the Associated Greeting Card Co. and she didn't want anything to happen to them – at any rate not until she had sold all the Christmas cards she possibly could and had her bicycle safely won. The boys and girls who started selling now would be a whole month behind Helen. Yes, she certainly had something to show for herself with the first batch of cards all sold and another lot asked for. It didn't really matter about the Boston Baby Hospital; she'd soon earn that money back again.

The sun was very hot and seemed much hotter on top of the fence. She started with 'The Lucky Sixpence' but it was hard to read because the print danced up and down on the page. She turned the other way round and hung her legs over the front so that the magazine was a little bit in her own shade. Then she leafed through the pages to the *St Nicholas League*, and suddenly remembered that she hadn't sent in any contribution for June. She had meant to decide on her subject that afternoon by the mill pond and had thought about 'A Good Beginning' which was the title for the story or essay. Then later, she had considered writing about a day that began with everything wonderful and ended in disaster as so many of them seemed to; so she tried to write about that very day at the mill pond. But, when she did, the bad part of the day was so much the most interesting and there was so little about the good beginning that it didn't seem to fit the title at all. She had meant to try again before the closing date, but there had been too many other things to think about. There had been Betty's illness, and then the excitement of selling the Christmas cards. In the end she had forgotten all about 'A Good Beginning'.

Now as Helen read over the new titles, she saw that the announcement of the winners for these July competitions wouldn't be made until the November number. With the hot June sun burning through the back of her cotton dress, Helen felt that November was an infinite distance away. It was most discouraging. If her poem for the September number wasn't good enough, then she had missed October and she would have to wait almost until winter for the results of this contest. The subjects for the verse were 'The Sentinel' or 'On Guard' but they didn't sound like much fun, Helen thought, for a girl to write about; and the story was even worse – 'My Favourite Hero (or Heroine) in History and Why'. If it had been just 'My Favourite Hero or Heroine' it would have been all right, but 'in History' made it like writing a lesson at school.

Helen shut her eyes to think about heroines in history and the minute she did, she knew that something was wrong because of a most frightening quietness. She opened her eyes quickly and looked over her shoulder. The playground was empty. A moment ago it had been crowded with children playing tag or sitting under the trees. But now there was no one to be seen anywhere. Helen climbed down from the fence and dashed into the building. How late was she? There were no girls in the dressing-room and from the classroom came the ominous sound of Miss Perkins's voice. The bell must have rung.

Helen tiptoed to the door and then tried to slip into her seat unnoticed, but Robert Busby coughed loudly, and then *St Nicholas* slid out from under her arm and fell with a rustling thud to the floor. Miss Perkins turned around from the blackboard and she didn't look at all pleased.

'It does seem to me, Helen, that on the next to the last day of school you could manage to behave sensibly like other children.'

Helen felt the hateful blush spread up her arms, her neck, and even into the roots of her hair. Someone whispered behind her and someone else whispered back, 'The Funny Guy – The Funny Guy'. It seemed to run around the room like an echo. Helen sat down and opened her desk. If only she could climb inside it and hide away from all the eyes. Why hadn't she heard the bell? Why hadn't someone told her? They all *wanted* her to be The Funny Guy. She could hear Susan giggling and another whisper behind her back.

'I really don't know what I'm going to do with you, Helen.' Miss Perkins sighed and turned back so that her next words were addressed to the blackboard. Helen liked this much better, but she didn't like what she heard. 'Well, anyway, I won't have to worry about you next autumn. You'll be Miss Hanscom's problem.'

Now everyone had something else to think about. Miss Hanscom was known to be the strictest teacher in the school. She was said to have kept a boy shut up all day in her store-cupboard and to have made blue marks on another boy's hands where she had hit him with her sharp ruler. But someone said the boy had painted the marks on with ink. All the same, on this next to the last day of school, the thought of changing Miss Perkins for Miss Hanscom was not a happy one.

Helen stood up. 'I'm sorry, Miss Perkins. I was on the fence, reading. I didn't hear the bell.'

'It's all right, Helen,' Miss Perkins said wearily. 'Now let us get on with this last lesson or Miss Hanscom will send all of you back to me and that would never do.' She turned around for a moment and smiled at Helen and then the lesson went on, and the rest of the day dragged by without any more serious difficulties.

That afternoon Helen decided to take her *St Nicholas* out under the oak tree in the back yard. She read 'The Lucky Sixpence' again but the rest of the stories, except the other continued one, 'The Townsend Twins', which she didn't like quite so much, all seemed to be about Fourth of July subjects. 'Books and Reading' was all about Nature books: moths, butterflies, insects, fishes, flowers, shrubs and mosses. Helen wondered if Betty Higgins liked that kind of nature book. She didn't like them much herself. Ernest Thompson-Seton's animal stories were much better, or books about trekking through the wilds. No, this was a disappointing *St Nicholas*, and there was no doubt about it. She threw it on to the grass and lay down on her back with her hands behind her head. She could just see one patch of blue sky through the thick leaves and when the breeze moved them a bright ray of sunlight shone across her face. She felt sleepy but she couldn't go to sleep because there were too many things to think about.

Tomorrow school would be over; that was the most important thing. Then she would have time to write her heroine story for *St Nicholas*. It must certainly be a heroine and not a hero, but who was there? She had once played the part of Mary Todd Lincoln in a play. She could do her, of course, but she wasn't exactly a heroine. It was really her husband, Abraham Lincoln, who was the hero. Then there were all sorts of brave women in the Civil War. Perhaps she could find one of them who wore her dead brother's clothes and went to fight like a man, or something like that. But these weren't her favourite heroines. The real ones never seemed to be as good as the ones in books; girls like Jo in *Little Women* or Carol in *The Birds' Christmas Carol* or Sarah Crewe. Who could she write about?

Suddenly she sat up. Betty Higgins would know. She was good in history and she would have hundreds of ideas. Mrs Higgins had said to be sure and come back and so had Betty herself. Helen dashed into the house to give the top of her hair two quick brush strokes. She couldn't take time to undo the pigtails and plait them over again even if they did look a little wispy. She tucked the *St Nicholas* under her arm and hurried out the front door. But by the time she had reached Birch Road, she had slowed down to a walk. Perhaps this wasn't a good time of day. It must be almost five o'clock. Maybe Betty had to have her supper early. Helen wanted to turn around and go home. Perhaps, if she just walked by number sixteen, Betty would be in the hammock and see her and call her in. But when Helen came close to the house there was no sound from the porch. She looked up at the front door and the windows. Everything was shut tight and the house had an empty silent look.

With a sudden spurt of courage, Helen turned in the path and ran up to the porch. There was no one there; and even the hammock, chairs and table had gone. This was too much like a bad dream. Helen pushed the bell anxiously and heard it ring far away inside the house. Then she listened for footsteps, but there was no sound. She rang the bell again, and kept her finger on it for a long time, but still nothing happened.

This was worse than anything Helen could have imagined. What had happened? Perhaps Betty had suddenly got worse and they had had to take her away to the hospital. Perhaps she would have to stay there for ever and ever like Helen's mother. Then, as Helen turned to walk slowly down the steps, she saw a piece of paper on the path in front of her. She picked it up and read the large capital letters saying – 'Milkman', and then, beneath them, 'Please don't leave any more milk until further notice.'

Well, that didn't help much, but it did sound as though they had all gone away. It didn't sound as if just Betty had gone to the hospital. Susan would know, of course, but Helen didn't want to ask Susan anything. Then she thought about Mr Walsh. If he was Betty's Postman, he would know all about where she had gone because he'd have to forward the mail. It was too late to find Mr Walsh now. Well, she would just have to wait until morning.

There was nothing else to do, so Helen went back to her desk and made herself write three hundred words about Mary Todd Lincoln. By the time she had finished, Auntie Cris was calling her to supper, and then, in no time at all, she was saying her prayers and thinking about her mother and father the way she always did at bedtime.

Auntie Cris had told her that her father had telephoned

after she had left for school in the morning. Why did it have to be the one day when she left early to stop at the Post Office and send the Christmas card money? Anyway, he'd left her a message to say that her mother was better but couldn't see anyone yet. He also sent his love and said he would be home for supper on Friday night. Well, Monday was over now and there was only Tuesday, Wednesday and Thursday to wait before she would see him.

With this comforting thought, she finally fell asleep.

CHAPTER TEN

Holidays Begin with Rain

THE last day of school was not even a whole morning and went by very quickly because Miss Perkins gave back all the old test papers and stories that had won gold or silver stars and all the drawings that had been good enough to hang around the room above the blackboard. Helen always had a great many gold and silver star test papers and stories but her drawings were not so good as Susan's. All the same, the pile on her desk looked very impressive and Miss Perkins noticed it and said, 'Good for you, Helen.'

Then in almost a minute, it seemed, they were all filing by the door to shake Miss Perkins's hand and to say 'Good-bye'.

It was sad to say good-bye. It always was if you liked your teacher and weren't going to see her so much any more. But it was good to leave the red brick building and know that you didn't have to think about it again until the thick green leaves had turned red and gold and begun to come drifting down. By that time all sorts of things could have happened. Helen shut her eyes and tried to imagine what it would be like to ride a bicycle to school every day and to wear a Silver Badge on her coat. 'Oh, that,' Helen would say when everyone asked her what it was, 'that is what I got for writing a poem. It's printed in the September *St Nicholas*.' Of course it wouldn't be so much fun to show the poem to Miss Hanscom but Helen could still visit Miss Perkins and show it to her.

Helen decided not to take the short cut home because

she had found one penny in her pocket which must have been left over from the ten cents Mr Walsh had given her for her birthday. She remembered now that she had only bought seven cents' worth of sweets after she got the stamp for the letter to her father. How long ago that seemed. But it was good to find even one penny after all the money troubles she had been having lately. She had decided to go by way of the station since there was plenty of time before lunch and there was a machine on the platform where you could put in a penny and get a stick of gum. As Auntie Cris didn't approve of chewing gum, Helen planned to sit on the bench by the tracks and wait for the eleven-fifty train from Boston to come in and go out. This was always fun to do, and it would give her time to finish chewing the gum before she went home.

It was lovely sitting there. The gum tasted deliciously sweet; there was no one else in sight on the whole length of the platform, and Helen had a great many important things to think about.

Perhaps next year would be better after all. Betty Higgins might even be her friend instead of Susan's. But where had Betty gone now? No one had said anything about her at school even when Miss Perkins had given Susan a pile of Betty's work to take for her. Well, Helen would just have to wait around for Mr Walsh when he came with the afternoon mail. The new Christmas cards couldn't possibly come from New York before tomorrow but there were plenty of things to do. 'My Favourite Heroine in History – Molly Todd Lincoln' had to be copied out and it would be fun to write a letter to Mother now that she was so much better. Maybe she would even be able to write an answer or get Nurse Brandon to write one for her.

These were all comfortable thoughts, but after a while

the gum began to have no taste left and it looked as if it might rain, so Helen decided not to wait for the eleven-fifty train.

As it happened, the rain held off until after lunch. But then, as Auntie said, it began 'in earnest' – not the quick showery kind but a slow steady rain that would go on and on without stopping. Helen finished her story, wrote her letter to her mother, then put them both in envelopes and addressed them. She would have to get Auntie Cris to sign the story as original and beg stamps from her but that would be easy because she would approve of both letters. After that Helen couldn't think of anything else to do and she had heard the church clock strike two, only a few minutes ago. Mr Walsh never came before half past three and usually it was later than that because Helen often met him on her way home from school.

Helen knelt down on the floor by the open window and watched the caterpillar rivers of rain on the screen. They wriggled and ran much faster than real caterpillars.

'Drip, drip dismal drip, drizzle drip, dismal drizzle drip,' Helen said out loud and the leaves of the oak tree made their faint rustle of agreement.

There wasn't anything to do. Betty had disappeared and Helen didn't want to see Barbara until the cards came. She would just want to play stupid baby games. No, it would be better to wait until they had the selling to do. Auntie Cris was having her forty winks, and Helen had heard her funny little snores before she closed the door and made her own room secret and quiet.

Well, she couldn't just sit and be dismal for a whole hour or more. She didn't have any money left to buy anything at Belcher's but she could go to the library and get some new books to read. She put on her old blue raincoat and pulled the hood up over her head. She even remembered to put on her rubbers.

There was no one in the library except an old man looking at an atlas, so Miss Singleton had plenty of time to tell Helen what she ought to like. As Helen had never once liked what Miss Singleton thought she ought to, she decided not to take any books at all. Instead, she sat at the big table to read magazines. She looked first at *The Youth's Companion* then *Little Folks* and in both of them she found the same advertisement of the Associated Greeting Card Co. and the same picture of a bicycle. That meant that hundreds and hundreds, maybe thousands and thousands, of boys and girls would be trying for one boy's bicycle and one girl's bicycle and it was all quite hopeless. What chance would Helen Hamilton have among millions of other girls and boys?

Helen pushed the magazines away and got up quickly.

'Aren't you going to take anything?' Miss Singleton asked.

'No, not today, thank you,' Helen answered much too loudly. Miss Singleton frowned and the old gentleman looked up from his maps.

The afternoon seemed to grow longer and longer. If the whole of the summer holidays went dragging by like this, she'd rather be back in school – she'd even rather be The Funny Guy than to be just no one in a great empty world. But as she passed the Congregational Church on her way home and looked up through the grey drizzle of rain, she saw that it was almost half past three, and when she turned into her own front path, there was Mr Walsh standing on the porch.

'I've got a most important question to ask you,' Helen greeted him even before he could speak.

'Well now, I hope I can answer it then.' He put down his bag and took off his grey-blue cap to shake the water off it.

'I want to find out about a friend who lives at number sixteen Birch Road –'

'Birch Road. Dear me, that's not on my beat. What's her name?'

'Betty Higgins, but I guess her real name is Elizabeth Higgins.'

Mr Walsh shook his head. 'I don't seem to know her but I think Tom Black does Birch Road and he's a good friend. I could ask him.'

'Oh, *could* you, please? I'll come back to the Post Office with you right now.'

'Dear me sakes, it must be dreadfully important,' Mr Walsh said. 'I'm afraid Tom'll be finished and gone home before I get to the Post Office. His beat's shorter than mine.' Then seeing Helen's face dripping with rain, and looking near real tears, he added, 'But I can ask him first thing in the morning. Now just what was it you wanted to know?'

Helen explained about the closed house and the milkman's note.

'Why, she's probably gone away for a little change of air with her family. I don't need to tell you that it's holiday time now.'

'Yes, and she was going to the seashore – only not for a while, and – and I was to go and see her first.'

'Yes, but with all that fine weather we had last week, I wouldn't wonder if they'd just packed up and gone. But they won't like this much.' He stared out at the cascade of water running off the roof and down the front path.

'Well, if she has gone, Tom, Mr Black I mean, will have a forwarding address, won't he, and you could get that for me and I could write to her.'

Mr Walsh pushed back his cap and scratched his head. His old eyes looked anxious as he stared down at Helen. 'I'm afraid I can't do that. The Post Office doesn't allow it. But I'll tell you what, I can find out if she has gone to the beach and then you can write her at home and Tom can forward it in the usual way.'

Helen felt discouraged. She'd have to wait until tomorrow to know whether Betty was really away or in the hospital. Then she'd have to write a letter and it would go so roundabout that it would take ages to get to Betty. 'Well, I suppose that's the best we can do,' she said.

'Come now, cheer up. The sun'll be out tomorrow and the whole world'll look different. Goodness me, with all this talk I nearly forgot to tell you. There was a letter for you. I put it in the letter box and then never gave it another thought. You run in and get the key and I'll get along home and change my wet clothes. I won't forget to ask Tom about your Betty Higgins and I'll ring the bell tomorrow and tell you what he says. That's fair enough, isn't it?'

Helen thanked him and said good-bye quickly. Then she hurried around the house to go in the back door.

Auntie Cris was sitting in the rocker. 'I thought I heard the Postman's knock,' she said.

'Yes, and there's a letter for me in the box. He said so. Quick, where's the key?'

Helen reached up to the shelf over the stove and felt behind the alarm clock.

'Mind, mind!' Auntie said, and then, 'Take off those rubbers and that dripping raincoat before you track all the wet through the house.'

'Oh, Auntie, must I, please? I'm in such a hurry,' Helen said.

'Of course you must. That letter'll keep. My rheumatism's real bad today and I'm not going around after you with the mop, and that's certain.'

Helen flung off her raincoat and struggled with her rubbers, then ran through the house and out on to the porch again. She could see the letter through the little slit in the front of the box. She wrestled with the lock and, in a moment, the door was open.

It must be from The Associated Greeting Card Co., she decided, and would probably say they had received the money and were sending some more cards. But it wasn't. It was addressed in round clear handwriting and the postmark was 'Quonset, Mass.'

Betty!

Helen tore open the envelope and read the two neatly written pages twice over before she could really think what they were saying:

Dear Helen,

I am here at Quonset with my mother; and daddy is coming tomorrow if the weather holds fine. We decided since I was so much better to come here quickly and I've been swimming already and it's lovely on the beach.

I didn't have time to tell you I was going so soon and I hope you didn't come to play with me and find I'd gone.

I'm afraid I won't be home again until just before school starts in September unless I have to go to Boston to the dentist. If I do, I'll come over and see you.

I wish you were here to play with me. None of the people are here yet that were here last year and I haven't met anyone else either so the cottage seems empty and strange. I wish you would write to me.

Love from,
Betty.

Helen folded the letter and put it back in the envelope. Well, anyway, Betty wasn't in a hospital and she must be much better or she couldn't go in swimming. It was awful to think that she would be away all summer, but she *had* written and she *did* wish she had Helen to play with. Helen wouldn't be going away anywhere at all because they couldn't go away until her mother was well and that wouldn't be for a very long time. So she would be sure to be at home if Betty did come back to go to the dentist. And, anyway, Helen would have to be working hard for the bicycle all summer. She decided to write to Betty that very night and then, in the morning, when Auntie Cris felt better, she would ask her for three stamps, one for her mother's letter, one for *St Nicholas* and one for Betty. Auntie Cris would be sure to approve of all three things.

Auntie Cris would have to sign about the Mary Todd Lincoln essay being original too. Yes, it would certainly be a good idea to wait until morning when Auntie Cris's rheumatism might be better.

But in the morning it was still raining – the same steady rain that looked as if it would go on for days and days. Auntie Cris didn't sing as she washed the breakfast dishes. She grumbled instead.

'Fine weather for your friend at the seaside. If I was her mother I'd turn around and come straight back home. I always did say it's no good counting on summer until we get past the Fourth of July.' As she spoke, she kept giving the mop fierce jabs into the dishwater.

'Oh, do you think they *might* come back home?'

'Staying with friends, are they?'

'No. It's their own cottage. But maybe if they don't like it, they might rent it to someone else and come back.'

'Not likely now. It's too late for renting.'

The doorbell rang suddenly.

'That must be Mr Walsh,' Helen said. 'He promised he'd ring and tell me about where Betty was, but now he doesn't need to.'

Auntie Cris dried her hands on the roller towel and sank into her rocker. 'Fetch me your nonsense to sign, and you can take three stamps from under my pincushion. But first you'd better ask Mr Walsh to come in and have a cup of coffee and a sit-down. I wouldn't be a Postman in this weather for anything. No, not me.'

As Helen ran to do all these things at once, she heard Auntie's last sentence turn into a little song:

'No, not me. I wouldn't be a Postman. No, not me.'

When Helen came back with the stamps and the letters, Mr Walsh was already drinking his coffee. He looked very large and round sitting in Helen's chair at the table.

'I found out about Betty,' she said quickly. 'That letter was from her.'

'I thought it might be. But this isn't very good weather for Quonset.'

'I was just saying the same thing to Helen,' Auntie remarked.

Auntie Cris signed the essay without reading it, and Helen was a little disappointed. She wished now she had waited for her father to sign it on Friday. There would still have been time, and it would be nice if someone thought what she had written was very good. But perhaps it helped to send things in early. She stamped the letters and, as Mr Walsh stood up, he took them and promised that he would send them off at once.

'Have you got a parcel for me?' Helen whispered as she went with him to the door.

'Not this morning. Most of the parcels come in the afternoon mail. Your Auntie said she was going to make strawberry jam. That ought to keep you out of mischief this morning.' He put on his soggy cap and went off down the path. Helen watched him until he was swallowed up in the grey misty rain.

The morning passed quickly. Helen loved topping the strawberries and the delicious smell of the kitchen on jam-making days. And in the afternoon two good things happened at once. The sun came out and the cards arrived. They were in a neat parcel with a letter and a record to show how many cards had been sold. 'Keep up the good work,' the letter said.

Very well, she would do just that. She would go straight over to Barbara Buckingham's house and not waste a single moment. The rain had stopped and there were two good hours before suppertime.

But when Maria went to find Barbara, Helen had to

wait a long time on the porch. At last the screen door banged, and Barbara came out.

'We can go right now,' Helen said. 'The new cards have come. I've got them here.'

'I can't go.'

Helen looked at Barbara for the first time and saw that she had been crying.

'Why not? What's the matter?'

'Nothing.'

'Please tell me.'

'I can't.'

Helen was worried. 'You didn't tell your mother, did you?'

'No, I did not. So there.'

'Well, why can't you then?'

'I just can't.'

'Well, can you go tomorrow morning?'

'No, I can't' – there was a long silence and then she added the one word – 'ever.'

'Oh, Barbara, *please* tell me what's the matter. *Please.*' Helen was near tears now. 'It's all so important. Don't you see?'

'All right then. You asked for it. I didn't tell my mother but Mrs Cadwalader Brown *did*. And my mother's *furious*. She – she says she's going to tell your father.'

'But why? My father wouldn't be furious. That is, I don't *think* he would be.'

'Oh, yes, he would. It's because of the Boston Baby Hospital. My mother said we were like common peddlers and then, when I told her about the hospital, she said it was' – Barbara hesitated, and then fairly shouted the words – 'FALSE PRETENCES.'

CHAPTER ELEVEN

Mrs Buckingham Interferes

'FALSE pretences, false pretences,' Helen kept saying over and over again to herself all the way home. But nothing seemed to make sense. She went in through the back door without slamming it and then up the stairs to her room.

Usually on the afternoon of a jam-making day, she would go into the pantry where the sweet-smelling jars were all put out on newspapers to set. It was part of the day's work to test the shining red moons with one finger and then suck off the delicious stickiness. But this afternoon Helen hadn't any heart for jam. Her world was full of troubles, and troubles, and more troubles; and the only thing for it was to hide away by herself in her own room and try to think everything out.

'I don't know what she means by *false pretences*,' Helen said aloud to a small bird who was trying to find shelter under the leaves of the oak tree. 'I wasn't pretending anything and so there couldn't be anything wrong about it. I did say I was selling the cards for the Boston Baby Hospital and I was. I will make up the money I spent as soon as I make more money and then I'll add a lot more, too.'

The bird shook his head suddenly and flew away. He's off about his business, she thought. Auntie Cris would say he didn't want to listen to my silly nonsense. She got up slowly and saw the old shopping bag with the cards lying on the bed where she had thrown it.

'I don't care. I don't care,' she said fiercely. 'I'll just show old Mrs Buckingham and Barbara, too. I'll just go and do it all alone and I'll have all the money and no one to bother me. I don't care if they do tell my father. He'll understand. He'll *have* to.'

She picked up the bag and went down the stairs as quietly as she had come up them. But as she walked along Hyde Street she decided to start her calls as far away as possible from Mrs Cadwalader Brown's house. Perhaps it would be better to go all the way to Centre Newton. It wasn't too far, and she still had enough time left.

The trees still sent down showers of raindrops when the breeze moved them but the sun made hopscotch patches on the sidewalk and Helen began to enjoy her private expedition. Centre Newton was a larger village than Newton Lowlands and Helen was glad she had made the long walk as there were plenty of houses very near together and it didn't seem to take any time at all to go from one to the next. At first she thought she would try not to mention the Baby Hospital but she soon found, as before, that no one wanted to buy any cards. Well, she would certainly have to earn the money she owed the Baby Hospital anyway. It would be worse than anything not to pay them at all. It didn't take long to decide that it would be best to do the selling for the hospital's benefit.

The magic worked again. The minute Helen said that she was selling the cards for the benefit of the Boston Baby Hospital, the packets melted away. And almost everyone was friendly and glad to see her. Even the people who stared at her crossly, holding the door open a crack, smiled when she spoke of the hospital and, as before, asked her to come in while they went to get the money.

At six o'clock, when Helen knew that she would have to hurry home or be late for supper, she had sold ten of her twenty-five packets. Two dollars and fifty cents jingled comfortably in the bottom of the shopping bag as she skipped happily along. It was much better to do the job all by herself, much better to have the money she didn't have to send to The Associated Greeting Card Co. to divide between herself and the Baby Hospital. She would start out again tomorrow morning as soon as Auntie would let her go, and, in no time, all the cards would be sold. Perhaps next time she would ask them to send fifty packets instead of twenty-five. She noticed that her shadow looked very long in front of her, as she came out into a sunny patch of road, so she ran the last few blocks. It was most important to keep Auntie Cris in a good mood now that Helen had the whole job of selling the cards.

But Auntie Cris was not in a good mood at all.

'Wherever have you been?' she asked crossly when Helen banged into the kitchen.

'I've been over in Centre Newton,' Helen answered without thinking.

'Centre Newton! Now what in tunket have you been up to way off there?'

'I was – playing with a girl at school.' The little lie slipped out before Helen could stop it.

Luckily Auntie Cris had her mind on something else and didn't bother to ask any more questions. Instead she said, 'Well, your father's been trying to get you on the telephone. He's called twice. And the second time, he *was* put out, I don't mind telling you. He said he had to go along to the hospital right away, but that he would call you at half past eight and you weren't to go to bed until he had talked to you.'

As Helen ate her supper, she kept thinking about what her father wanted her for. Mrs Buckingham couldn't have told him yet – or could she? Anyway Helen felt sure she could explain that it wasn't false pretences. Even now she had earned fifty cents. She owed the Baby Hospital twenty-five cents of it for the first cards sold and ten cents for the ones she had sold today. So already she had fifteen cents of her very own money and this time she wouldn't buy a single ice-cream soda, or even one piece of candy.

'Eat up your supper, Helen, and stop mooning. I want to do these dishes and get my old bones to bed.'

'Aren't you going to wait up for father to telephone?'

'Yes, but it's nearly eight o'clock now. Eat that nice rice pudding and stop marking up the tablecloth. I really don't know what I'm going to do with you. You're more bother than six sensible children.'

'Am I very different from other children?' Helen asked. The awful thought had sometimes occurred to her that she might really be a funny guy and that Auntie Cris and her father and mother all knew that she was odd but were too kind to tell her, the way Robert and Susan and the others did.

'You're different enough to want shutting up in a zoo. I'm all tuckered out and tired with your antics and goings on.'

Helen said no more; and she did hurry through her rice pudding without picking out the raisins to eat last. Auntie Cris never approved of this, and tonight she might be crosser than ever.

They were just putting away the last few dishes when the telephone bell rang.

'There now, you run along and answer yourself. It's sure to be your father. I'll just tidy up here, and then I'll be up in my room if he wants to speak to me.'

Helen raced into the study, grasped the telephone fiercely and held the receiver to her ear.

'Hello! Hello!' she shouted.

A woman's voice said, 'Is that you, Helen?'

'Yes.' For one moment Helen thought it just might be her own mother got miraculously well. But when the voice went on speaking she knew that it couldn't possibly be anyone but Mrs Buckingham.

'Is your father there?'

'No,' Helen said in a voice that didn't sound like her own; and then added, 'I think he's in the hospital seeing my mother.'

'Well, I'm sorry to have to bother him at this time but I think he ought to know how you have been going about ringing doorbells like a common peddler. I'm sure he wouldn't like it at all.'

'I don't think he would mind,' Helen said slowly.

'Well, I do, and, even if your mother is ill, I must have a word with him about it. When will he be home?'

'Not until Friday night,' Helen said.

There was a pause and then Mrs Buckingham said, 'Very well, I'll have to telephone him in his office tomorrow morning.'

'Oh, please –' Helen started to say, but Mrs Buckingham rang off without waiting for her to finish.

Helen hung up the receiver and stared at her father's pipes in their old familiar rack on the table. Oh, dear, she thought, if only she'd wait and let me tell him first. She'll make it all sound so awful.

The telephone rang suddenly and Helen jumped. Of course, she'd forgotten. Now she could tell him.

'Well, Nelly,' her father's voice answered her 'Hello'. 'Wherever have you been? I've called you twice. You must certainly have been late for supper.'

Helen thought he didn't sound angry – only very tired and far away.

'I'm sorry, Daddy. And I do want to tell you what I was doing. You see, in St Nicholas there was an advertisement to sell Christmas cards –'

'Nelly, dear, I can't stop to hear about it now. I've just run out from the hospital for a few moments while the doctor is seeing your mother. I'll be home for supper Friday night and we can talk about everything then.'

'But Barbara Buckingham's mother said – ' Helen tried to explain.

'Please, Nelly. It will all have to wait. I must go now. I only telephoned because your mother wanted to be sure you were all right. She's had your letter and she was very pleased. She is getting stronger every day and wants to see you, but the doctor says not for another two weeks.'

'Two weeks – ' Helen forgot all about the Christmas cards and Mrs Buckingham. Two weeks was too long to wait. She couldn't bear it. 'But Daddy – '

'Now, Nelly, you must be a brave girl. I have told you that you must be patient and good. You're very lucky to have your mother getting well at all – '

'Oh, I know I am. But, Daddy – ' Helen felt choking tears, and for a moment she couldn't speak.

'It can't be helped, Nelly. We must do everything the doctor says. You know that and you're not a baby any more.'

Suddenly Helen remembered that she *had* to tell him about the Christmas cards before Mrs Buckingham did. 'I've got to tell you something right now. It's very important.'

'It can wait, Helen. I really can't talk any more now. I must go. Good night, dear, and love from your mother and from me.'

'Good night, Daddy,' Helen said quietly. It was no use. Even if she did make him listen he would be bothered, and he wouldn't try to understand. No, there was nothing to do except try to explain on Friday. But, by then, Mrs Buckingham would have made everything sound wrong.

The door opened and Auntie Cris came in.

'I thought I heard the telephone ring twice,' she said.

Helen started to say that Mrs Buckingham had telephoned, and then she stopped just in time. If Auntie Cris knew about everything she would be so cross that she wouldn't let Helen sell any more cards at all. Helen thought quickly and another lie came very easily. 'The first time it was Daddy, too,' she said, 'but we got cut off and he had to ring up again.'

Helen blushed and turned away quickly. Auntie Cris looked at her suspiciously for a moment and then, to Helen's relief, said,' Well, now you run along. It's past your bedtime. You can come down to my room when you're ready and then you can tell me what your father had to say.'

'It wasn't much,' Helen said, 'but I will come down and I'll get ready as quick as I can.'

'That's a good girl,' Auntie Cris said. 'Now run along,' she said again.

Helen fled up the stairs and, to her joy, found a mound of round black kitten curled up in the middle of her bed.

'Oh, Cindy,' Helen cried, putting her face down against his soft warm fur. 'If Auntie Cris saw you here she would spank you hard. But she won't see you. I won't let her.'

Cindy purred, stretched and then started to curl back into his tight ball. Helen rubbed him under his upturned chin. 'Oh, Cindy,' she said. 'Everything – every single thing is all more wrong than it's ever been before. And I can't see any way that it will ever be right.' Suddenly she threw herself down on the bed and put her head close to the little cat who continued his throaty purring. And then the tears came, floods and floods of tears.

'Helen, HELEN, aren't you ever going to get ready for bed? Where in tunket are you?'

Helen jumped up, blew her nose fiercely, and hurried out of her clothes and into her nightdress.

'Will you stay for the night with me, Cindy?' she asked the now silent kitten on the bed. Cindy opened one green eye and winked at Helen sleepily. And then, suddenly, he jumped up as if he had been shot from a cannon like the clown at the circus.

The reason for Cindy's hurried departure was soon explained. When Helen turned around, she saw Auntie Cris standing in the doorway.

'So that's what you've been up to all this time. Playing with that plaguy cat. It's a good thing I climbed all those stairs. Now you get straight into your bed.'

'I – I haven't washed yet, nor said my prayers.'

'Very well. Go and wash and I'll stay right here until your light's out.'

When Helen was safely in bed, Auntie Cris reached up and turned off the gaslight. 'What did your father have to say?' she asked, not unkindly, but she did not stoop down to kiss Helen good night.

'That mother is better but – oh, Auntie – I can't see her for two whole weeks.'

'Two weeks. That's no time worth mentioning. When you're my age you won't notice the difference between two hours and two weeks. They're all one to me.'

'Oh, I know, Auntie, but I'm not your age and they're two years to me.'

'Nonsense. Go to sleep now, and mind you get up when I call you in the morning, and don't bring me over these stairs again.'

When Auntie Cris had gone, Helen lay awake for a long time trying to decide what to do. The best thing would be to start out early and sell all the rest of the packets of cards. There were fifteen of course, and they might take the afternoon as well as the morning. But, if

there was time, she could go to the Post Office and get two money orders – one for five dollars for The Associated Greeting Card people and one for fifty cents to send to the Baby Hospital. It would be as well to get that done quickly and not wait until she had a dollar. Then everything would be all right before she had to talk to her father about it. Yes, and there would be a little money left for herself even after she had paid for the postal orders and the stamps. Maybe she would have enough to buy a real present for her mother – a sort of homecoming one – something really big – like a beautiful brooch or a new carpet-sweeper.

With these comforting thoughts Helen fell asleep. But all night long she kept dreaming that Mrs Buckingham had turned into Mr Punch and was chasing after Helen with a great stick – up and down, up and down, in and out – through all the streets of Centre Newton.

CHAPTER TWELVE

A Prisoner Escapes

AUNTIE CRIS wanted to finish the strawberries before they got too soft, and Helen had to help with the topping so that it was nearly eleven the next morning before she could leave the house. Moreover, it was a very warm morning and the long walk to Centre Newton seemed endless. By half past twelve Helen had to start back home for her lunch. She was hot and tired and very cross because she had sold only five more packets of cards.

When Helen had dried the dishes after lunch, she looked longingly at the cool shade under her oak tree in the back yard. Then she remembered that today was Thursday and that the cards must be sold and the money paid before she saw her father tomorrow night. She turned her back on the oak tree and went upstairs to get the cards and the shopping bag. Then, all the long way to Centre Newton, she helped herself to forget how far it was by singing, *Onward, Christian Soldiers.*

And, at last, the familiar round of calls began again. She went wearily from door to door, saying over and over and over again: 'Please will you buy some Christmas cards for the benefit of the Boston Baby Hospital. Please will you buy . . . Please will you buy.' Sometimes they did, and more often, in the sticky afternoon heat, they didn't want to bother with anything. But, at last, every packet had been sold and, as Helen passed the church in Centre Newton on her way home, the deep-voiced bell announced that it was six o'clock.

Helen brushed the stray hairs back from her forehead

and tried to plait the pigtail that had come undone, but her hands were so sticky and fumbling that she couldn't manage it. Even the jingle of the coins in the shopping bag didn't cheer her very much. She hadn't finished in time to get to the Post Office, and now what would she say to her father when he telephoned, as he was sure to do, if Mrs Buckingham had caught him in his office, and as she had said she would? It wasn't much use hoping that she hadn't. Helen felt quite certain that Mrs Buckingham would succeed in doing whatever she set out to do.

The news that greeted Helen when she got home confirmed her worst fears. Auntie Cris was silent as she put down Helen's supper on the red checked cloth and Helen was silent too. She was almost too tired to care.

But quite suddenly Helen was wide awake and listening to Auntie Cris's dreadful words.

'Your father telephoned this afternoon. He's told me all about this wickedness you've been up to. You are a deceitful girl to lie to me about it. Ringing doorbells, peddling through the streets – I can't think what got into you –'

'I –' Helen started to explain, but Auntie Cris cut her short.

'No, don't interrupt. I'll have my say and be done with it. Your father is very upset and I don't know what he thinks of me letting you get up to such tricks. But I'm just too old to look after the likes of you, Helen Hamilton, and if your mother doesn't get better soon you'll be the death of me.'

Auntie Cris looked so fierce, and unlike herself, that Helen couldn't bear it. She clutched her hands tight together under the table and stared down at the untasted poached egg on her plate.

'Your father can't get back here until tomorrow night

like he said. Tomorrow you're to be kept in my sight all day.'

'Can't I even go downtown to the Post Office?'

'No. You heard what I said. You aren't to be out of my sight all day. Now, eat up your supper.'

But Helen couldn't eat anything and, after a while, Auntie Cris gave up trying to make her.

Before Helen went up to bed, she made one more effort to soften Auntie Cris. 'Is there any way I can telephone to father? I haven't had a chance to explain to anyone. You all just listen to Mrs Buckingham and she only knows what Mrs Cadwalader Brown and Barbara told her. It isn't really fair.'

But it was no use. '*Fair*. Don't talk to me about *fair*. You've just been going your own way behind my back. You're a fine one to talk about being *fair*. You go to bed now. Your father'll see you tomorrow night and he's much too busy and worried to have you telephoning him. And that's that.'

Helen went to bed but she couldn't sleep. Never had the whole world been so empty. There was no one – no one anywhere who would understand how everything that she had meant to be good and wonderful had turned out to be bad and sinful.

She turned on one side, and then on the other, but she couldn't get away from the black thoughts and the tight pain of wanting to cry and being too miserable even to let the tears come. The bed seemed to get hotter and hotter until, at last, she couldn't bear it another moment. If she couldn't sleep it would be much better to kneel in front of the window and look out into the darkness.

But the night wasn't dark. It was bright with moonlight and the oak tree danced and shimmered as if it had been lit with fairy lights. It was so lovely that it made Helen remember part of a poem that her father had read to her:

Lo! the moon ascending!
Up from the East, the silvery round moon;
Beautiful over the house-tops, ghostly, phantom
 moon;
Immense and silent moon –

Then, thinking how much she had loved being with
him and hearing his voice, she remembered that he was
angry with her and that he might never forgive her or
read to her again, and that he had given her no chance to
explain.

The tears came slowly at first and then faster and faster.
Helen never knew how long she sat crying by the window.
But, when the storm was over, she felt better. She looked
out at the dancing tree, and then the Great Idea came to
her.

She wouldn't let herself be a prisoner all day; she
wouldn't wait to be scolded by her father. She would run
away – now – before Auntie Cris began to watch her. If
she ran away and never never came back, perhaps they
would be sorry then.

Once she had thought of the Great Idea, Helen began
to plan just how she would escape. She went to the door
and listened. Yes, Auntie Cris was fast asleep and snoring
steadily. Well, the first thing to do was to find out what
time it was, and the best way to find out was to go down
and get the alarm clock in the kitchen. The stairs seemed
to creak and groan as she tiptoed down them, and she kept
stopping to listen for the reassuring snores. It was very
dark except on the landing where the moonlight made a
bright patch on the worn red carpet, turning it to silver.
She stopped for a moment to look out at the world on the
other side of the house and then hurried down to the
kitchen.

The journey back was worse. The tick of the clock was
so loud that Helen was sure it would wake Auntie Cris.

She hugged her nightgown around it as much as she could, and it seemed to protest even more at this treatment. But nothing happened and, at last, she was safely back in her room with the door closed behind her.

Helen put the clock down gently on her desk and, beside it, the box of matches that she had found near the clock on the kitchen shelf. She wasn't supposed to light the gas herself but she often had, and what did one small sin matter when she was lost in a whole world of sin and despair?

With great care, Helen stood on the bed and lit the gas. The clock said only quarter past eleven. How could it be so early? Surely it must be morning by now. Helen was sure she had been awake all the night long. But the clock was ticking as loudly as ever and Auntie Cris always said it never lost more than five minutes in a whole week.

Well, this discovery meant a change of plans. Helen couldn't go out now and have all the night to wait on the station platform for a train. The first one that went into Boston in the morning left at ten minutes past five. Helen knew this for certain because everyone knew about the milk train. She had taken it once with her father when they had gone for the day to see some of his cousins in New Hampshire, and had had to take a train from Boston that left the North Station at eight.

Suddenly Helen yawned. The best plan would be to set the alarm for four o'clock and have a little sleep first. Then she would just have time to get dressed and slip away to the station. Yes, that was the best plan. Auntie Cris would never hear the clock with both doors closed.

Helen was dreaming that she was swimming in a lovely green sea when the alarm bell rang out. She had left the clock on the desk on purpose so that she would have to get up to turn it off. And, once up, she remembered the exciting plan and hurried into her clothes. She could see the familiar objects in the room by the faint grey light of early morning, and she didn't have to light the gas again.

Money was the most important thing. But there was plenty of money in the bottom of the shopping bag. If she was going to run away for ever it didn't matter about The Associated Greeting Card Co. or about the Boston Baby Hospital, either. Six dollars and twenty-five cents would take her hundreds of miles away. Then she could get a job as a waitress, or helping in a store, or as a nursemaid and pay back everything she owed. She would have to borrow it for now. It was her only way of escape.

As the money was in silver, she had great difficulty in getting it all into her purse, but she could just manage to shut the clasp and put it safely into the button-up pocket of her raincoat. She looked out of the window anxiously. The sky was lightening behind the oak tree, and it was probably going to be a fine day. Still, she must take her raincoat as there were sure to be rainy days.

This reminded her of the problem of clean clothes. She would only take a few, since she could buy some more when she was earning plenty of money. She packed the old shopping bag carefully. She was wearing her new pink dress which was almost clean as she had only worn it once, to church on Sunday. Then she put in another dress, some underwear, her bathing suit, since she just might go somewhere near the seashore. Then she went to the bathroom very quietly, and collected her toothbrush, and washing things.

Back in her room, she looked at the clock and saw that it was only half past four. It wouldn't take more than five minutes to get to the station, so she decided to make her bed and write a farewell note.

It was hard to see to write and the words seemd to sit on top of each other when, afterwards, she held the paper up to the window to look. Well, it didn't matter much, except what she had written at the end, and that was quite clear. Nothing mattered except that. She could not give her love to Auntie Cris, nor even any to her father. They had made themselves into her enemies. They were the ones she was escaping from.

On her way out, Helen put the clock and the matches back on the kitchen shelf and helped herself to two doughnuts from the jar in the pantry. She ate one quickly and put the other in a paper bag inside the top of the shopping bag in case she was hungry later. She would have liked to say good-bye to Cindy but he wasn't in his basket by the stove and she didn't dare to call him for fear of waking Auntie Cris. She unlocked the back door quietly and let herself out.

A few minutes later, as she sat on the station platform watching the sky turn pink behind Mr McGerrity's barn on the other side of the railway tracks, she felt suddenly frightened. Wouldn't it be better to go back while she still could? No. Never. Perhaps the empty feeling was just hunger. She ate the other doughnut and then, before she had time to think again, the train came puffing into the station. The conductor helped her up the steps and she

stood by the iron gate for a moment to watch the baggage man hoist the milk cans up into the front car. Then, as the engine began to puff out of the station, she went back to find a seat. There was no trouble about that. The carriage was quite empty. She looked out of the window and the frightened feeling was gone.

The adventure had begun.

At half past eight, Auntie Cris began to wonder why Helen didn't come down for her breakfast. Well, let the child sleep if she wanted to. There wasn't any school to worry about and what in tunket would the child do with herself all day? The jam was finished. Perhaps she could help make a pudding for supper or some of those cookies she liked so much. Or she could go out in the garden. Mr Hamilton hadn't said 'no' to that. 'Just as long as Helen doesn't go out of sight of the house,' he'd said. Auntie Cris sighed heavily. She was much too old to look after a youngster like Helen.

Auntie Cris began to think about her own Johnny. He'd been up to tricks, too, but she'd kept him in order, no mistake about that. Perhaps that was the trouble. Discipline was all right, and children who didn't have it came to no good. She'd always believed that sparing the rod spoiled the child. All the same, she didn't much like the idea of being a gaoler even for one day. Auntie Cris sighed again, and got up to pour herself another cup of coffee.

As she did, she saw that the clock said nine o'clock. No child should lie abed after nine. She went out into the hall and called up the stairs, 'Helen – Helen – Helen.'

But there was no answer.

'Plague take the child,' Auntie Cris muttered. Well, there was nothing for it but to climb the stairs.

At the landing she stopped and called again but there was still no answer.

When Auntie Cris opened the door to Helen's room she stopped for a moment to catch her breath, and then she looked around her.

The sun streamed in across the pink roses on the carpet and climbed sideways up the bedspread on to the carefully made bed.

The bedspread! The carefully-made bed!

There was no sign of Helen. The room was quite empty.

Auntie Cris sat down on the small chair by Helen's desk and felt her old heart pounding away against her ribs. She couldn't believe it. How had she gone? Where had she gone?

And then she saw the note on the blue blotting paper on the desk. It was sealed up in an envelope and printed on the outside were just two words, 'Auntie Cris'. Her hand trembled as she tore it open and managed to read the note inside, though some of the words seemed to be written on top of each other:

Dear Auntie Cris,

I have decided to run away because I don't want to be in prison even for a day and no one will let me explain and everyone thinks I am different from other girls and wicked at heart. But I am not.

Do not try to follow me. I will be far away when you read this and I am not coming back – ever!

from Helen.

P.S. Please give my love to Mother. I would only be a burden to her so it is better for me to go.

Auntie Cris sat quite still with the note in her hand. She was remembering another day, years ago, when she had found a note from Johnny. But Johnny had been a grown man. Surely Helen was only hiding somewhere. She couldn't go far without any money. Well, it wasn't any good sitting here. She'd better search the house and see if the child wasn't up to some of her tricks.

But there was no sign of Helen anywhere.

At ten o'clock Auntie Cris went to the telephone and called Mr Hamilton's office.

'Don't you worry, Auntie Cris,' Helen's father said when he heard the story. 'It's my fault, not yours. She can't have gone far in this short time without any money.'

'I've been thinking about that,' Auntie Cris said. 'What about all those Christmas cards she was selling? She was out the whole day yesterday.'

Mr Hamilton groaned, and then he tried to be re-assuring, but Auntie Cris was not easily reassured. 'I keep thinking about my son that ran away,' she said. 'He's never been seen from that day to this. Vanished into thin air, as the saying is.'

'Now, Auntie,' Mr Hamilton said quietly. 'Helen is twelve years old. People will notice her all by herself. We'll find her in no time at all. You go and make yourself a cup of coffee and just be there in case she comes home of her own accord. Then you leave the rest to me.'

With this, Auntie Cris had to be satisfied. She went back to the kitchen and tried to think what to do.

Mr Hamilton hung up the receiver and turned to his secretary. His face was grey with anxiety and for a moment he didn't speak.

Miss Evans looked at him. 'It's Helen, isn't it? Run away, has she? They will do that at her age. My sister's kids are always dashing off. Mark my words, she'll be back before the day's over.'

'I wonder if I'd better call the police,' Mr Hamilton said uncertainly.

'I wouldn't. It'll only get into the papers and one of the nurses is sure to tell Mrs Hamilton.'

'No, we can't let that happen.'

'I'd just wait if I were you. Someone's sure to be on to you soon.'

But by lunchtime there had been no call, and even Miss Evans had begun to show signs of anxiety. Mr Hamilton decided to have a sandwich and coffee in the office. Miss Evans brought them in to him and then said she would slip out and get her own lunch if he didn't mind.

Mr Hamilton was glad to be alone. He wanted to think quietly, and the more he thought, the less he liked his own thoughts. The trouble was that he had been too busy and too worried to think about Helen at all. He put his head in his hands and pushed his sandwich away.

CHAPTER THIRTEEN

Punishment

HALF PAST eleven was the best time for swimming at Quonset, when the tide was high. And on this Friday morning in June, the sun was warm and the tide was at its highest. The beach swarmed with children who ran in and out of the water, while more sedate grown-ups sat on the sand and watched, or ventured carefully into the waves.

Inside the Higginses' cottage, Betty struggled into her bathing suit. This was the happiest moment in the day and, now that she was well again, everything was more fun. She went to the window as she tucked the last strands of her hair up under her bathing cap. It was wonderful having a cottage right on the beach. She loved it now when the sand lay bright in the sun, and she loved it even more when the big storms came in the autumn and the waves washed right up to the front door.

All her friends had come back again now, the same friends that she had known every summer for as long as she could remember. She hurried into her sand-shoes, reached for her dressing-gown, and then bounded down the stairs two at a time.

And at that very moment the doorbell rang. It was probably the butcher's boy with the meat.

'I'll go – ' Betty called out to her mother who was in the kitchen.

Betty opened the door and stopped still with surprise. It wasn't the butcher's boy at all. It was Helen Hamilton.

'Helen!' Betty said because she couldn't think of anything else to say. And then she added quickly, 'Hello,' and 'Do come in.'

'I've just come to see you,' Helen said in a very small voice.

'That's good,' Betty said. 'Will you stay for the day? Have you brought your bathing suit?'

Helen could only manage to nod dumbly in answer to both of these questions. Of course, she hadn't meant to come to Quonset at all, but then she had seen the train in the station and well, then, she just had come – and when she got out at Quonset, she hadn't meant to come to Betty's house, but it was so easy just to ask and then it had been so near. Now when Betty seemed glad to see her it made a great lump come into her throat and she couldn't say anything at all.

'Mummy – Mummy!' Betty called. 'Helen's come.'

Mrs Higgins came out of the kitchen, drying her hands on her apron. She looked at Helen for a moment and then said, quietly, just what Betty had said, 'Did you bring your bathing suit?'

Helen nodded again. She still couldn't speak.

'Well, dash up to Betty's room and get into it. You'll just have time for a good swim before lunch.'

In ten minutes Helen and Betty were on the beach and Helen had forgotten everything except the fun of being there with Betty.

'I'm sorry I didn't tell you I was coming. I – well, I just thought of it suddenly.'

'I'm glad you did. I was wondering if it was awfully hot in Newton Lowlands. But you must have had to get up terribly early to get here so soon.'

'I did. I took the milk train.'

'The milk train! But that goes at five o'clock in the morning, doesn't it?'

'Ten minutes past.'

Betty looked at Helen for a moment and then she laughed. 'I never really understood why we all called you The Funny Guy at school, but I can see now.'

But the way she said it was all right. Being funny didn't matter if people laughed with you and let you laugh too. Helen grinned but she couldn't think of anything to say. She couldn't possibly tell Betty about running away.

But Betty wasn't even interested any more. 'Come on,' she said, 'the others are all in the water. You can swim, can't you? Come on then – '

Mrs Higgins looked at the clock on the kitchen shelf and saw that it was after one. The girls would be up from the beach any moment now. She added another chop to the two she had laid out on the table and then rolled up a few more cinnamon buns, but her mind wasn't on what she was doing.

'I wonder,' she said aloud, and then, again, 'I wonder – ' There had been something defiant about Helen as she stood there on the porch and said nothing to explain why she had come. She must have got up very early to get to Quonset on the morning train. Perhaps it would be a good idea just to make sure that her father knew where she was.

Mrs Higgins rubbed the flour off her hands and went out into the hall to the telephone.

She knew that Helen's father was a lawyer and she was relieved to find him listed in the Boston telephone book. The call went through quickly and the conversation she had with Mr Hamilton was a short one. She went back to the kitchen slowly and thoughtfully.

'Well, anyway,' she said aloud to the rolling pin, 'she'll have had a good swim and a good meal – poor lamb.'

At lunch, Helen and Betty talked excitedly about their swim and about their plans for a game of Hare and

Hounds in the afternoon. Helen's face was shining and her eyes were very bright. Her pigtails had been undone to let her hair dry and her pink dress had a few dark spots where the water had dripped on to it.

She looked so happy that Mrs Higgins could hardly bring herself to say the things she had to say.

'I'm afraid there won't be time for Hare and Hounds this afternoon,' she said quickly.

'Why?' Both girls asked the question at once.

'Well, I wanted Helen's father to know that she had arrived safely, so I telephoned him at his office.'

Helen put down her fork quickly and the bright colour drained away from her cheeks.

Mrs Higgins hurried on. 'He says she must catch the afternoon train back. It goes at 2.50, you know.'

'Must I?' Helen asked in a choked voice.

'I'm afraid you must, dear. Your father is going to meet you in the South Station and take you home. You'll get to Boston just before six.'

'Oh,' was all Helen could say. She shouldn't have come to Betty's. But it had been such fun. And now it was all over for ever. And whatever would happen to her? What would her father say?

'You'll have to come again, now you've found the way,' Mrs Higgins said quickly.

'Oh, Mother, why can't she stay one night now she's here? You brought your things, didn't you, Helen?'

Helen blushed and nodded. She hadn't meant to let Betty see all the things in the shopping bag but she had had to get them out to find the bathing suit which was right down at the bottom.

'I'm afraid not, dear. Mr Hamilton wants her to come home now and I think he's right about it.' She looked directly at Helen for the first time and Helen looked down at her plate. 'Come now, we won't talk about it any more.

149

You eat up your lunch, and then we'll all walk over to the station together.'

But Helen wasn't hungry any more. Everything had tasted so good but now even the cinnamon bun seemed to stick in her throat. She would have to go back. She couldn't run away any more. Mrs Higgins would put her on the train and her father would be there at the other end to meet her. Even if she got out somewhere on the way, he would know where to look for her.

But on the train, Helen began to think about getting off at one of the stations before the train got to Boston. Perhaps she could hide; and she still had a little money left. Her father would be angry; and now she had added hundreds of new sins on to the other one. And these were real sins: – running away from home, not telling the truth, and, worst of all, using up the money that belonged to The Associated Greeting Card Co. and the Boston Baby Hospital.

The conductor was calling a station now. Helen got up and reached for her shopping bag and then she sat down again quickly. No. It was no use. It would be better to face the music and get it over with. Even if she had to have days and days in prison. Even if Mrs Higgins would never let her play with Betty again when she knew the whole truth. Even if the worst happened and God punished her by making her mother die. Even then, she would have to face it and live her whole life through being sorry and trying to be good. Two large tears dropped down on to her hand and she wiped them away quickly.

'Piece of chocolate, Miss?' The man on the other side of the aisle reached across and handed her half a chocolate bar.

'Thank you,' Helen said. She had been told not to speak to strangers. But what did that matter now unless, of course, the chocolate was poisoned or had something in it to make her sleep so that he could kidnap her? She looked across at him sideways. He didn't look at all like a kidnapping kind of man. But then they were apt to look nice in order to fool you. Still what did it matter? If he kidnapped her, then she wouldn't have to go home. Then she would be properly lost for ever. She ate the chocolate quickly and was surprised to find that she felt much better.

A few moments later, it seemed, the conductor was calling, 'South Station, *South Station*. This way out, please.'

Helen was the last person to climb down from the carriage. The man from across the aisle turned back to smile at her, and hurried away. Then all the passengers who had been in the carriages behind pushed by. At last there was no one left and Helen stood alone on the platform.

There was no sign of her father. A porter pushing a loaded barrow pointed to the gate and when Helen walked on she saw her father standing just behind it.

'Hurry, Nelly,' he said, as she came near. 'Your train is a little late and you seem to be the last person to get out of it. We've got just two minutes to get the Lowlands train – '

Helen ran along beside her father to the track at the other end of the station where the familiar little train was puffing and snorting and getting ready to start.

'Hop in here, Mr Hamilton,' the brakeman said. He was standing at the back of the last carriage and he looked anxious.

Helen climbed up in front of her father and they found a seat together. Mr Hamilton put Helen's shopping bag and his briefcase on the rack over their heads and told Helen to move into the seat by the window. Then he sat down and opened his paper.

Helen started to speak but the words choked in her throat.

Her father did not look at her, as he usually did. But he said quietly, 'You and I have a great deal to say to each other, Nelly, but we're not going to say it now in a crowded train.'

He went on reading his paper and Helen looked out of the window quietly. They did not speak again until the train was puffing under the bridge before the Newton Lowlands station.

'Here we are,' Mr Hamilton said as he got to his feet and reached for the things on the rack.

His voice sounded quite natural and ordinary, Helen thought, and not in the least cross. She followed him out of the train in silence.

Auntie Cris stood at the door as they walked up the path.

'Well, Missy,' she said, 'you've decided to come home, have you, after all?'

'We won't talk about anything now, Auntie,' Mr Hamilton said. 'Helen has a great deal to think about.'

Helen didn't want to think about anything. She tried to smile at Auntie Cris but her face felt stiff.

'Well, your supper's ready. You'd better get off upstairs and take that train dirt off your face.'

Helen was very glad to escape. Her room looked exactly the same as when she had left it. A light breeze lifted the curtains at the window and the oak tree was whispering outside. The note had gone from the desk.

At supper Mr Hamilton talked to Auntie Cris. He asked her if it had been hot in Newton Lowlands and then said it had been 'very close' in town. Auntie Cris told him that the winter coal had come and that she had signed for it.

There was creamed chicken on toast, Helen's favourite food, but Helen couldn't eat it. She kept wondering what her father would say and when he would say it. The worst

thing of all was that she had used almost all of the Christmas card money. And now that she was at home the police
would find her when The Associated Greeting Card Co.
didn't get their money. There was no escape. If she could
get some more cards without paying for the last, she could
send back the money, but even that wouldn't be enough
and, besides, now that Mrs Buckingham had made such a
fuss she was sure her father wouldn't let her go on selling
cards – not ever –

'Eat up your supper, Helen. I made this especially for
you,' Auntie Cris said.

'I'm not hungry,' Helen answered. 'Perhaps I have a
temperature.'

'A little sunburn, I expect,' Mr Hamilton said. 'But I'd
have thought that sea air would have given you an appe-
tite.'

'I ate a great big lunch,' Helen said.

'Well, you eat up your supper now,' Mr Hamilton said,
and so firmly that Helen did eat it up. When the last bite
was finished, she felt better.

As soon as the meal was over, Helen was sent up to get
undressed. Mr Hamilton took his paper into his den but,
before he closed the door, he said, 'When you are in bed,
I'm coming up to see you, so knock on my door when you
come down to say good night to Auntie Cris.'

Now that the time had come, Helen wanted to get the
talk over. She hurried into her nightdress and in ten
minutes was knocking at her father's door.

'You go on upstairs. I'll be up in a few moments, Nelly.
I want to ring the hospital and see how your mother is.'

Helen lay still waiting for her father to come. He
seemed to take a very long time and it was almost dark
when, at last, she heard his slow step on the stair. She was
rather glad about the darkness. It made it easier to talk.

'Well, Nelly,' her father said, after Helen had moved

over to make room for him on the edge of the bed, 'shall we begin with some good news?'

'Oh, yes, please.'

'The doctor happened to be at the hospital when I called just now, and said he wanted to talk to me. That's what took so long. He says that he now knows the operation has been completely successful and that your mother is going to be quite all right again.'

Her father's voice was very solemn, and Helen could hardly believe that it was such good news that he was telling her.

'Yes,' he went on, 'if she goes on at this rate, she'll be able to come home in September.'

'In *September*.' Helen repeated the magic words. September was the month she had been looking forward to most. Betty would be back then and her *Song of the Woods* might be printed in *St Nicholas*. Now she would be able to show it to her mother.

'Yes. I hope I can take her away to Atlantic City, or somewhere bracing, for a week or two in August. Then she ought to be all right.'

'Will – will I go, too?' Helen asked without thinking.

'No. I'm afraid not this time. Your mother will have to have a very quiet holiday and it wouldn't be much fun for you.'

'Oh, but it would, Daddy,' Helen had completely forgotten all her troubles.

Her father was silent for a moment and then he said, 'Now, Nelly, what have you got to say to me?'

Helen turned her head into the pillow and a muffled voice said, 'I am sorry. Oh, I am sorry, Daddy. I didn't think.'

'I'm glad you're sorry, but I think it is time you did think. Now just take your face out of the pillow and tell me all about everything from the very beginning.'

And suddenly Helen wanted to tell her father everything – about being called The Funny Guy and about not really having any friends at school until Betty Higgins was suddenly so nice that day at the mill pond. And then about the Christmas cards and the bicycle and Mrs Cadwalader Brown and Barbara and Mrs Buckingham. All the troubles and wrong things and right things came pouring out into the darkness while Mr Hamilton listened without saying a word.

At last Helen stopped talking and, after a minute, Mr Hamilton reached over and felt for her hand.

'I think I'm to blame for a great deal of the trouble, Nelly – '

'Oh, *no.*'

'Don't interrupt for a minute. If I had had a little more time to talk to you, we could have worked out all these problems together. Or if your mother hadn't been ill for so long. But we can't overlook the fact that you have done wrong, and that you, and no one else, have got to make that wrong right.'

'How can I?' Helen asked, and her voice sounded far away and as if it belonged to someone else.

'Tomorrow morning before I go to the office I will write a cheque for The Associated Greeting Card Co. How much do you owe them?'

'Five dollars.'

'Well, that's a great deal of money for one girl to earn. But you will have to earn it, Nelly – every penny.'

'By selling more cards?'

'No. I don't agree with Mrs Buckingham about very many things, I confess, but I do agree with her that selling Christmas cards under false pretences is not what I would expect my daughter to do – '

'But I was going to give some of the money to the Baby Hospital – '

'Yes, but very little. And you let everyone to whom you sold the cards think that all the money was for the hospital, didn't you?'

'I just didn't think.'

'No. Because it was easier not to. Well now, you will have to give me what you have left and earn the rest of the five dollars you owe me and, I think, an additional five dollars which you can send to the Baby Hospital when you have earned it.'

'Ten dollars! But, Daddy, how can I ever earn that much?'

'I've been thinking about that. I was going to hire Danny, to get the garden and the lawn looking nice for your mother's return. But I think I won't get Danny, after all. It is almost the first of July. You will have two full months, and if you work for a while every day, I will pay you five dollars to give to the Boston Baby Hospital on the first of September and your debt to me for what I have paid your greeting card company will be paid, too.'

'I know I can do it,' Helen said after a moment. She felt suddenly happy.

After a moment her father went out. 'Of course you can do it, but it won't be easy; especially as I'm not going to give you any pocket money for spending. That is going to be your punishment, Nelly. Whenever you want money for anything, stamps or pencils or sweets, you will have to come and ask me for it. You won't like that at all. But you will learn the value of trust if, for a while, you aren't trusted. Do you understand that, dear?'

'Yes.' Helen's face went back into the pillow.

Her father stroked the back of her head gently and then he stood up. 'Turn right-side-up now so I can kiss the tip of your nose.'

Helen turned right-side-up quickly and, after her father had kissed her and started to the door, he turned back to say, 'You know I don't think there is going to be any Funny Guy in the eighth grade. Something tells me that there isn't.'

And then he was gone.

CHAPTER FOURTEEN

The Debt is Paid

ON a very hot August morning, Helen was weeding the shadiest part of the garden. It hadn't rained for nearly a week and the soil was packed hard so that when she pulled the long grasses and weeds that poked their heads above the thick lily-of-the-valley leaves, they broke off in her hands. It was discouraging. She picked up the trowel and tried to pry the point down between the roots, but all that ever seemed to come up were the nicest lily-of-the-valley plants. A mosquito hummed angrily around her head and as she slapped at it another dirty streak appeared on her hot face.

Less than half the bed had been done, and Helen knew that, if it were to rain, the grasses and weeds would pop up again in the part that looked all right now. She had learned, in her summer's work in the garden, that every single piece of root of every single weed had to be pulled up and burned or stuffed into the waste bin, or the hateful thing would come back again larger and higher than ever. She sighed heavily and shoved the old box cover on which she was kneeling to a fresh patch of weeds.

'Blast those Katzenjammer Kids,' she said suddenly in a very loud voice.

'Blast who?' a voice said directly behind her.

Helen turned around quickly but there was no one to be seen anywhere. Then she saw a flash of checked gingham behind the trunk of the oak tree.

'I can see you, whoever you are,' she said slowly, and her hot face felt even hotter as the blush spread upward from her neck to the roots of her hair. If it was Susan, or one of her gang, they would remember what she had said and, of course, it was a very Funny Guy thing to say.

But it was Betty Higgins who slipped out from behind the tree.

They looked at each other for a full minute before either of them said anything. Then Betty asked again, 'Blast *who*?'

Helen pushed a pigtail back over her shoulder and hoped the blush would go away. 'Oh, that's just a thing I read in the comics once and I always say it when I can't bear what I'm doing. It seems to help just to say *something*.'

'Yes, I know. I've got a thing I say, too. Only mine is "*Oh my Ears and Whiskers.*" You know, what the White Rabbit keeps saying in *Alice* – But what's the matter? What are you saying yours now for?'

Helen looked at Betty. Her skin was a lovely golden colour and she had freckles across her nose and all up and down her arms. 'Oh, nothing much,' she said quickly because she didn't want to explain about the summer job, even to Betty. 'I thought you were at Quonset.'

'Well, I am. I mean, I was. Mummy had to come up for a day and she brought me with her. We came last night.'

'Why?' Helen couldn't imagine anyone leaving Quonset for even a day, and right now the thought of the cool green waves and the delicious sound of the sea were almost too much to bear.

'I needed some new sandals and I had to go to the dentist. I told you I might. But that wasn't the real reason.'

Helen waited, but when Betty didn't explain, she had to ask.

'It's a secret just now,' Betty said and then she laughed. 'But I think you may know tomorrow.'

Helen was too hot and tired for secrets. It was wonderful to see Betty after having no one except Cindy to play with all summer. But Betty looked so happy and cool. She didn't have to work. She didn't have a mother who was ill. She didn't have any troubles at all. 'I don't care if I do know or don't know,' she said.

Betty saw how hot and tired Helen looked and she said quickly, 'I've got the rest of the morning before I have to go into town with Mother. Can I help?'

'No. You'll get all dirty.'

Helen was so glad to see Betty that she couldn't understand what made her cross. She wouldn't have blamed Betty if she had stamped and sulked and gone home the way Barbara Buckingham always did, but Betty only said, 'It doesn't matter if I do because this is a play dress. I've got to change it anyway. What are you doing – weeding?'

'Trying to,' Helen said, 'and I *must* get this bed done this week. It's the last one and when it's finished the garden will be all ready for when Mother comes home.'

'When's that?' Betty asked.

'She's going with Daddy to the White Mountains tomorrow to get strong and then she's coming back with him the Sunday before school starts – that's two weeks from the day after tomorrow.'

'I know because that's when we're coming home – ' Betty started to say something else and then changed it to, 'You know if you wet that bed with the hose, the weeds would come up a lot quicker.'

'I never thought of that,' Helen said, looking up at Betty with new respect.

'Well, let's.'

Helen and Betty worked together for the rest of the morning. During the weeks since Helen's unexpected visit to Quonset, they had tried to write letters, but they had both been too busy to tell all their news. Now, as they worked, they talked, and by the time Auntie Cris rang the bell for lunch, they had forgotten that there was ever a time when they had not been close friends.

'I've got to dash,' Betty said, 'but, anyway, the old bed's done.'

Helen looked down and realized, for the first time, that what Betty said was quite true. There wasn't a spear of grass nor a dandelion head nor a single weed above the thick green of the lily-of-the-valley leaves. She was so surprised that she didn't say anything.

'You won't have to blast the Katzenjammer Kids this afternoon, will you?'

'No.' Helen laughed. 'Can you come back this afternoon? We could swim in the mill pond, or play.'

'I can't. I've got to go into town right after lunch and then we're taking the four o'clock back to Quonset with Daddy.'

'Oh – ' Helen looked down at her grubby hands and wished she could put the morning back again.

'But anyhow,' Betty said, 'the summer's almost over, and your mother's coming back.'

163

'Yes,' Helen said, but even now she didn't quite dare to believe it.

Betty ran off down the path, calling 'Good-bye' over her shoulder.

She doesn't really mind a bit, Helen thought. She's going back to her friends at the beach and I was just a filler-in for this morning. I hate her. I just hate her, she – but she knew she didn't hate Betty even for one moment, and she suddenly felt ashamed. She had never had a friend like Betty before, and even school would be different now. She picked up the tools and walked slowly to the back door.

'How did you get mud all over your feet, I'd like to know?' Auntie Cris asked crossly. 'Wipe them good before you come into my clean kitchen.'

Helen looked up at Auntie Cris's face. It looked very red and hot and little beads of sweat stood out on her forehead. But Helen didn't care whether Auntie Cris was tired, or cross. She felt tired and cross herself.

'I will if I want to,' she said rudely.

'Now, Missy Miss, none of that smart talk from you.'

Helen wiped her feet on the mat outside the door and pushed by Auntie Cris into the kitchen. She didn't speak again until she had reached the Floating Island stage of lunch.

'What's got into you?' Auntie Cris asked at last. She had moved over to her rocker and was fanning herself with the *Boston Herald*. She looked cooler and much less cross. 'I made your favourite dessert, Floating Island, and you haven't said a word about it.'

Helen felt cooler and less cross, too. 'I'm sorry,' she said. It's just that Betty was here this morning – and – and –'

'Come over here and sit on the stool by me.' Auntie Cris's voice sounded comforting and friendly. 'There,

there,' she went on when Helen was settled beside her, 'you needn't think I don't know. I've seen you working every day and getting to look like a plucked chicken. I've told your father I thought it was high time you had a little *holiday.*

'I wish I could go with them to the White Mountains.'

'You will next year. But it wouldn't be so much fun this summer. Your mother's got to be taken care of like a piece of Dresden china – yes siree – a piece of Dresden china – ' Auntie Cris made a little tune and began to sing softly, 'Yes, siree, yes siree – a piece of Dresden china – yes siree – '

Helen put her head down on Auntie's large soft lap, and, in two minutes, she was sound asleep. Five minutes later, Auntie Cris's singing faded away like the choir moving out of church into the vestry. Her head went back against the worn top of the old rocker and presently she began to snore gently.

It was fully an hour later that the telephone rang. Auntie Cris started up suddenly, nearly knocking Helen's head off her lap. But Helen jumped up too and ran to the telephone.

'I'll answer. I'll answer,' she called over her shoulder.

She came back to the kitchen a moment later to announce, 'It's Daddy. But he wants to speak to you first, and then I'm to talk to him afterwards.'

Auntie Cris got up slowly from her chair. 'Goodness gracious me,' she groaned, 'I'm as stiff as a poker. Fancy us going to sleep like that without the dishes done, nor the table even cleared away. Whatever are we coming to?'

Helen hopped up and down on one foot. She wanted to say, 'Oh, hurry, *hurry*, do.' Her father's voice had sounded as though he had a special secret and she couldn't wait for her turn to talk to him.

But to Helen's disappointment, Auntie Cris said, 'You stay here and clear the table then.'

Oh, well, her turn would come. But Helen had cleared the table and stacked the dishes before Auntie Cris came back. Helen took one look at Auntie's face which seemed to be shining with pleasure and then she ran to the telephone.

'Well, Nelly,' her father said. 'Mrs Higgins and Betty have just been in to see me.'

He paused and Helen said, 'Oh.'

'They wanted to know if you would like to have the last two weeks of your holidays with them at Quonset.'

'Oh,' Helen said again. But this time it was much louder and Mr Hamilton must have known all that it was meant to say, because he went on quickly.

'I've just been talking with Auntie Cris. She says she thinks you deserve a real holiday and she'll get you ready to go the day after tomorrow.'

'Oh, Daddy,' Helen said. And then, 'It's wonderful. I was just having a dream and now it's come true.' Then a dreadful thought came to her. 'But what about the garden – and the grass? It won't be nice for when Mother comes home.'

'I was looking at it this morning and I think you really have done a fine job of it. So we'll call our debt settled and I'll get Danny to keep an eye on things while you're away. When I get back with Mother, I'll give you the five dollars to send to the Boston Baby Hospital, so you won't need to think about that any more. And Auntie Cris says you deserve to have a little money of your own to spend so we'll take care of that when I come home tonight.'

'Oh, Daddy, it's all so perfect.'

'Yes. I agree. Well, you run along now and talk to Auntie Cris. I've got to write Mrs Higgins a note to say when you'll be coming and I've a lot of last minute things to do. Well, good-bye, Nelly. I think your mother and I will have a much happier holiday knowing that you're having one, too.'

Helen danced back to the kitchen.

Auntie Cris turned around from the sink.

'You don't look so peaky now. I wonder what's come over you,' she said.

'Oh, Auntie Cris. If it hadn't been for what you said, he mightn't, he just *mightn't* have let me go.'

'I don't know about that. Well now, come along and help me with these dishes. We've got a lot to do between now and the day after tomorrow.'

CHAPTER FIFTEEN

St Nicholas and a Letter

AT Quonset, one sunny day followed another until Helen lost count of them. She had several letters from her mother and father who were having, they said, a lovely time and fine weather in the White Mountains but were looking forward to getting back to Newton Lowlands. Helen was looking forward to that herself, though she hardly had time to think about home at all because there was always so much to do at Quonset.

But she had been wondering about the September *St Nicholas*. Auntie Cris had promised to forward it and it should have come almost at once. A whole week went by before, at last, Helen came up from the beach one day to find *St Nicholas* and a letter. She took them both up to her room, tore off the wrappings of the magazine, and turned quickly to the *St Nicholas League*. Her wet hair fell forward into her eyes and dripped in slow drops on to the open page.

She read what the Editor had to say about the drawings being the best entries this month with two gold and five silver badges won. 'Close behind the artists,' the Editor went on, 'come the poets of the League, whose contributions, always good, maintain their usual high standard of excellence. The mysticism and romance of the great forests, the solitude and grandeur of leafy boughs and shady dells, are voiced with rare feeling in many bits of exquisite verse, under the title "A Song of the Woods".'

At the bottom of the page was what Helen was looking for – 'Prize Winners, Competition No. 151.' But her name wasn't there. Anne Torry in Providence, Rhode Island, had won a gold badge and four people had won silver badges. But there was no mention of Helen Hamilton at all. Helen leafed through the *League* pages quickly. No, her poem wasn't printed. For a moment Helen's hopes were raised high but then they were dashed again. In *The Roll of Honour* at the end there was an *Ann Hamilton*. But it was definitely Ann, and not Helen, there was no doubt about it at all. Helen Hamilton's name didn't appear anywhere, even in *The Roll of the Careless* at the very end. Of course they must have received her contribution because she had got the League Badge and leaflet way back in May. Helen looked out of the window at the children playing on the beach and then back again at the disappointing page and at the water dripping down from her hair in little splashes.

The screen door slammed and Betty called, 'Helen,' and then, louder, 'Helen, where are you?'

But for a moment Helen couldn't call back in answer. She still couldn't believe her name wasn't *somewhere*. Her poem was just as good as the ones they had printed. She was sure that it was.

A step sounded outside the door and Betty said, 'Oh, there you are. Why didn't you answer me? You're not mad, are you? I just stayed to talk to Mary – She – ' Then Betty stopped and looked at Helen. 'Why, whatever is the matter with you?'

To her own surprise, Helen burst into tears.

'You – you haven't had bad news, have you?' Betty asked. She came nearer and then stopped. 'A letter, I mean, or – or anything.'

'No. It's only just *St Nicholas*. You see – ' And then Helen sobbed out the whole story.

'Here, let me look,' Betty said quickly, reaching for the magazine.

'It's no good. It isn't there. Not one single word about it.'

'No, it isn't. But I do know you have to try and try to be good enough to get in. Susan's tried for years and years – '

'Susan?'

'Yes. Didn't you know that?'

'No.'

'Well, I don't think it'll be hard to beat Susan. Look, let's do this month's, both of us, while we're here. It says in the rules you can compete whether you're a subscriber or not. I'll do a drawing, I think. The subject's "Through the Window" and I'll do the beach from here.'

'I don't care if I never do another thing.'

'Silly,' Betty muttered. But she was now busy looking through the rest of the magazine. 'There's a good life-saving story in here – "Surfman No. 7" – did you see that?'

'No – '

'Lunch is ready,' Mrs Higgins called. The two girls jumped up and it wasn't until that moment that Helen remembered the letter which had fallen on to the floor. She stooped to pick it up and Betty said, 'Is it from your mother?'

'No,' Helen said, frowning at the quavery letters. 'Why – it's the same writing that's re-addressed *St Nicholas*. It must be Auntie Cris.'

'Well, that's not important then,' Betty said. 'It'll be about how hot it is in Newton Lowlands, and Cindy and the garden. Come on, Mother wants us to hurry up, and I'm starved.'

Helen was starved, too, and that was why she didn't read Auntie Cris's letter until after lunch.

Dear Helen [it said],

You were right about the weakest link. Mrs Prouty was it. I went to call the very day you left and I *did* find a letter. It was from my grandson, Edward George McCrillis who says he's come to New York to study about automobiles and airyplanes. He lives in Australia, and his father, that's my Johnny, has a Livery Stable there and he, I mean Eddie, has got a mother and a sister about your age. But I'll tell you all about that when you come home.

Now here's the thing I want to say. Eddie's been here to see me and he only went back this morning. He came right off when I wrote to him, all the way from New York by the boat. He's a nice boy, all right, if I do say it whose my own grandson. Well, he's so glad about your telling me about the weakest link and finding me after all when he'd all but given up that he's found you a *bicycle*. He has a friend who has a garage and they're fixing up one all ready for you when you get home.

With love from your loving,
Auntie Cris.

'Oh, Betty,' Helen said. 'Oh – it *isn't* just about Cindy and the garden. It isn't at all.'

Betty looked up from *St Nicholas*. 'What is it, then? I was just reading about the aeroplane – It says – '

'Never mind what it says. Just listen to this.' Helen read the letter out loud slowly, and then looked up to see a puzzled frown on Betty's face.

'Whatever is it all about?' Betty asked. 'I mean the weakest link and all.'

So Helen explained about Auntie Cris's long lost son and about how they had talked about him, and, in the end, Betty was as excited as Helen.

'Do you know, Eddie ought to read this article called "The Aeroplane" I've been reading in *St Nicholas*. Just listen to what it says:

Less than eight years ago the aeroplane was unknown except to a few men who were conducting experiments in secluded parts of the country. The aeroplane is an American product having been demonstrated as practicable by the Wright Brothers, when others were first awakening to the possibilities of such machines. The Frenchmen – '

'Oh, don't read any more of that now,' Helen broke in. 'We'll show it to Auntie's Eddie, of course. But right now there are so many other things to talk about. And anyway, your mother wants us to go down to the drug store and get some ice-cream for supper.'

Betty put down the magazine, and grinned at her friend.

'Well, what are all the important things you wanted to say?' Betty asked when they had started off down the road.

'Have you got a bicycle?' Helen asked quickly.

'Well, I've got an old one that belonged to my sister – '

'I didn't know you had a sister.'

'Well, I have. She's married and she lives in California. She was going to the Rockies with us only I couldn't go.'

'You will next year.'

'Yes, and Daddy says maybe you can come too.'

'Oh!'

'But I wasn't supposed to tell you yet.'

'Never mind.' Helen was so excited that she couldn't even remember what she had been saying. 'About the bicycle – ' she said, at last.

'If I can get the chain fixed, we can ride together. I didn't bother because Susan didn't want to ride, or her mother wouldn't let her or something.'

'Let's not talk about Susan,' Helen said suddenly. 'You

173

know, I'm almost glad now I didn't get my poem in *St Nicholas.*'

'I am, too, because, if you had, you'd be ahead of me.'

'Well, I did send in one more thing, but I don't expect it will be any good either.'

'I hope not.' Betty laughed and Helen laughed back. 'Why don't you want to talk about Susan?'

'Because of – Oh, because it reminds me about school and – The Funny Guy.'

'Did you honestly eat that inchworm?' Betty asked suddenly.

Helen felt the hot blush starting behind her ears. 'Yes – yes, I did.'

'Whatever for?' Betty put the question quickly, and added, 'Don't tell me if you don't want to.'

'Oh, I do. Only – well, you see, it sounds so silly. I expect I wanted to be brave.'

'Brave? I thought you were just showing off. We all thought so. And then Robert or Susan said you were a funny guy – and that's what we thought you were. I did, too.'

'But you don't now?'

'No, of course not. But I still don't see why you had to be so silly. It was a crazy thing to have to be brave about.'

Helen wanted to explain to Betty and somehow it seemed very important to make her understand. 'Well, you see, last year everything went wrong all at once and when I was thinking about the things that were wrong I used to forget what I was doing and do silly things and you all laughed at me. So when Robert dared me to eat the worm, it seemed like a sort of test. The kind of thing that you have to do in fairy tales to break a wicked spell. So I ate it.'

'Didn't it taste awful?'

'No. I like sorrel leaves and that was all I could taste. Besides it didn't take long. I don't suppose eating a worm is really any worse than eating – a fish, or a cow, except that they've been cooked.'

They were both silent for a while and then Betty said slowly, 'I did think in a kind of a way that you had a lot of nerve. I couldn't have eaten it – even if I'd had to be killed instead. We all felt like that, I guess. So when Susan called you a funny guy, we all joined in. It's so easy to think what everyone else thinks, isn't it?'

'Yes,' Helen agreed. She knew now that Betty would make everyone else forget that there had ever been a funny guy.

Helen gave an extra skip to get into step and swung Betty's hand hard.